MADNESS FROM THE SEA:

THE DREAMLANDS

JONATHON T CROSS

That Spooky Beach

Visit us online at www.thatspookybeach.com

Madness from the Sea: The Dreamlands
Copyright 2024 Jonathon T Cross

All Rights Reserved

ISBN: 979-8-9883520-3-7

Connect with Jonathon T Cross at
https://x.com/JonathonTCross
https://www.facebook.com/jonathontcross

Interior Layout:
Lori Michelle
www.theauthorsalley.com

Also by Jonathon T Cross

There's Something Here From Somewhere Else

Madness From the Sea
Cthulhu's Lure
The Dreamlands

PROLOGUE

CTHULHU WAS RELEASED from the depths on March 23rd, 2025, unleashing chaos upon all who entered his domain. Word spread to every corner of the globe. Although the creature was dismissed at first as nothing more than a shared delusion, the truth made itself known via satellite imagery and eyewitness accounts.

Military forces assembled, the wealthy went underground, and the rest of the world braced for the end times. But the end never came. Cthulhu remained on R'lyeh, leaving humanity to wonder what his presence meant for their continued existence.

Despite humanity's nuclear surplus, military scientists feared the ramifications of bombing an interdimensional portal. So, in the two decades since Cthulhu's release, humankind has left R'lyeh untouched, choosing to live alongside the creature rather than risk a war that can't be won.

Meanwhile, the call of Cthulhu persists, luring victims by the boatload to R'lyeh. It's theorized that their sacrifice keeps Cthulhu sated and confined to his risen city. While an entire generation has grown up, untouched by the memories and experiences of the world that once was.

On every continent, societies prepare their young against Cthulhu's telepathic reach. Teaching them to resist the allure of R'lyeh, lest they be swayed to their doom.

Bad dreams and monsters under the bed are no longer scoffed at, they are active threats to humanity's survival.

No one is exempt, no location is beyond reach, not even the depths of one's mind are off-limits. The frailty of humankind has never been on grander display.

Membership in occult organizations has spread. Strange rituals designed to communicate with creatures from beyond Earth have become commonplace. Fanatics pursue Cthulhu's call, yearning to be possessed by dreams and united with their distant ruler, while others desire nothing but to be left alone.

Irrespective of their proclivity, all individuals must acknowledge and respect a new truth: thoughts are the grandest weapon yet devised.

FINN

FINN WITNESSED A kaleidoscope of vibrant, cosmic hues interwoven with deep, velvety shadows. Celestial bodies, peculiar constellations, and swirling nebulae painted the heavens before him in indigo and violet, while floating islands danced amongst the clouds.

Positioned in the sky, he cast his gaze upon the world below, as a deity would. Vast settlements dotted most of the flatlands. Beside them grew extensive and dense forests, beset by glorious mountain peaks. There were crystalline waters throughout, beautiful seas enclosed by land masses with channels in between.

Finn knew nothing of this world, or why he was positioned above it, but he didn't feel the need to question such things. Despite the peculiarity of his trance-like experience, he felt at home, suspended in the air, watching over these foreign territories.

That may seem an unusual stance, but the world into which Finn was born had always lacked the comfort of a warm welcome. Humanity was strange to him. The chaos, the hate, the unnecessary violence.

Everyone else was drawn into the madness, but the older Finn grew, the more disconnected he became. People's motivations were trivial, their mannerisms alien. He harbored no belief of superiority. Only the knowledge that he was irreconcilably different, and no matter how hard he tried, he would never experience the sense of belonging to which others were born.

As Finn contemplated his isolation, he failed to see the clouds parting. It wasn't until a blinding light passed through, washing over him like a heavenly beacon, that he took notice. He peered directly into the radiant beams, and they responded with a haunting symphony of cosmic echoes.

Shadows danced in his peripheral vision as a figure eclipsed the light—a young woman whose presence disturbed his tranquility. He was perplexed as to the cause, yet he felt a sensation pulling at his inner being. The woman instilled a sense of imminent disaster that belied her angelic appearance.

Being immobilized, Finn was vulnerable. He attempted to regain control of his faculties; however, his limbs were paralyzed. He was but a specter, unable to intervene as she drew nearer, walking along an invisible platform in the sky.

The woman did not speak her name, nor move her lips, but Finn sensed she was known as Nyar. She bridged the gap between them, stopping so near he could feel her presence. His extremities flooded with pins and needles.

But before he could utter a word, lightning shattered the sky. Thunder rattled his bones. No longer was he a hapless observer. Now he could sense the chills running down his spine and feel the thud of his heart as it collided against his ribcage. A cacophony of emotions flooded through him as he fell victim to Nyar's gaze.

Fear and sadness mixed with anguish, suffering, and dread brought tears to Finn's eyes, then melancholy, grief, and despair stole the air from his lungs. He dropped to his knees, clenched his fists, and cried out as rain poured from the heavens.

"What is this!?"

Nyar remained mute, pointing to a mountain below. Then she dragged her fingertip across the sky, tearing a hole in the fabric of existence. Beyond the breach lay madness, the likes of which Finn had never seen, nor sensed, and in the dark shadows lurked malevolent

4

entities—shapes that writhe and shift, formed from the very essence of nightmares.

"Stop, I beg you," Finn insisted, unable to bear the grief. "Please."

Nyar spoke at last. "The nightmares you have witnessed are yet to breach, but it is an inevitability which will unleash unspeakable horror."

"What are you talking about?"

"You must locate and seal the rift before it's too late."

Finn pressed his eyes shut, then flinched as a heavy textbook thudded onto the desk next to him.

"Wake up, Finn." Professor Hartfield stood overhead with his arms crossed. "In this academic institution, attendance is voluntary. If Cthulhu's effect on the contemporary world doesn't interest you, you're free to leave."

Finn was relieved to hear the derisive laughter of his peers. It was but a dream, a manifestation of his own vulnerability.

He had enrolled in this course because he wished to understand Cthulhu, the deity who had plagued the world since his birth. To help those afflicted by the call, to quell the ever-growing madness in society and avenge the memory of his father.

"Cthulhu is the only thing that interests me, sir. I'm here to make a difference."

"Wouldn't that be delightful?" Professor Hartfield scoffed. "The aspiration to save the world is shared by many, but the commitment required is often lacking."

"Maybe he's getting the call," a classmate suggested.

Professor Hartfield eyed the student, and with a sigh of resignation said, "Finn, I am obligated to evaluate you when anyone proposes the call."

"I understand."

"Are you experiencing any peculiar sensations?"

Finn wiped the perspiration from his brow. "No."

"Have you witnessed anything you can't explain?"

"Um . . . no?"

"Are you in need of further evaluation by the school's call counselor?"

Finn shuddered; students who went to the call counselor were rarely seen again. This dream didn't align with what he had read of Cthulhu's call, anyway, but admitting to an unusual experience was liable to get you institutionalized.

His own mother had gone mad from the call, and his father fell victim to cult violence before his birth. Suffice it to say, Cthulhu had been haunting Finn his entire life, and Finn wasn't about to let the deity take away his freedom.

"No further evaluation is needed, sir. Just lacking sleep."

The professor made his way to the front of the room to resume his lecture. "The call is no laughing matter, students. Never underestimate Cthulhu's lure. Through manipulation, he can possess the mind to believe most anything, and any vision, no matter how pleasant, can turn deadly."

"Are there pleasant visions?" Finn asked.

"A phenomenon that has received little attention," Professor Hartfield said. "Perhaps you can address it in your research paper." The professor concluded his lecture with a call to action. "Numerous scholars have speculated about Cthulhu's intentions, with many positing that he exists in a dual state of wakefulness and dreaming. Many have tried to decipher the call. Who amongst you can crack the code?"

The students slammed their textbooks shut and shuffled out of the room, but Professor Hatfield's words hung in the air.

Finn couldn't bear another vision, not with Cthulhu at the helm. He feared the intensity of his dream, how it overrode his conscious command, holding him captive in a world that surpassed the complexity of even the strangest minds.

Deep down, he knew his mother was the only person he could confide in. She was a woman who embraced unconventional solutions, never hesitated to provide her unique perspective, and thought little of authority. Perhaps her lived experiences could guide him through this nightmare. If only he could summon the courage to face her.

EMMA-LYNN

EMMA-LYNN STARTED HER day the same way she always did, alone. As she lay in bed, she stared at the dream catchers dangling above her, while visions of her late husband lingered in her thoughts. She turned onto her side, holding back tears as she pushed herself upright. It had been twenty long years since her husband's tragic death, and still the memories haunted her.

She collected the dream catchers one by one and brought them outside, hanging them on a clothesline like laundry, so the morning sun could evaporate their captured nightmares. Did she truly believe in Ojibwe mythology, and the Spider Woman who captured bad dreams with magically woven webs? Perhaps not, but nothing was certain these days.

It wasn't just the dream catchers which made their way into her daily routine, as evidenced by the salt circle surrounding her bed. Stuffed into her tear-stained pillowcases were dream pillows filled with rare herbs and reeking with the overbearing scent of lavender. Beside them, hand carved figurines stood guard on her bedside table, embodying the protective traditions of their respective cultures.

Emma-Lynn returned to her bedroom, ignited a bushel of sage, then fell to her knees, and closed her weathered eyes in prayer. She prayed not to a single God, but rather to the universe. To anyone or anything that might be listening.

8

Her prayers had yet to be answered, but she lived in an enormous world, and amongst suffering that saw no reprieve. That something good was out there offered comfort and a chance of friendship in an otherwise solitary existence.

Aside from her daily journeys to and from the clothesline, Emma-Lynn stayed indoors with her blinds drawn, the muffled sounds of the outside world barely reaching her ears. Her skin, lined with the age of two decades of mourning, had taken on a pale and sickly hue, indicative of the malnutrition and deficiencies which plagued her health.

She owed her life to a crew of Cthulhu victim-advocates who came by with weekly donations, although the rotted food they left on her stoop was less than required to persist. Part of her wished they would let her perish.

Wouldn't it be nice to be one of the lucky ones? She would ask herself. *People who live without the fear of destruction and chaos.* But much like the third world problems she had thought little of in her younger years, society cast a blind eye to the struggles of "the called."

So, when Emma-Lynn heard an unexpected knock at her door, she was filled with equal parts fear and curiosity. Her latest delivery of rotten vegetables had been dropped off only one day prior, and the advocates weren't due back for a week.

She made her way downstairs and peered through the peephole lens, hoping to identify her visitor before opening the door. Alas, they were standing out of sight.

Sometimes it was a salesperson, more often it was a cultist recruiting for their misguided flock. But there were worse visitors, people who wished to eliminate "the called." To foster a race of humans who possessed genetic immunity against telepathic manipulation. A ritual culling, as it were.

In her current mindset, Emma-Lynn cared little about the danger. She turned the brass doorknob and was greeted by the last person she expected to see.

9

THE REUNION

THE HAUNTING SCENT of burnt sage assaulted Finn's nostrils, like forgotten whispers of a bygone era seeping through the open door. In this olfactory seance, he straddled two lives. The childhood he wished to forget, and the future he couldn't bear to face. Standing before him, looking just as confused as he felt, was the proprietor of this condemned house, his mother, Emma-Lynn.

"Can I help you?" she asked with the callous detachment of a stranger.

Finn stared at his mother, absorbing the pained expression in her stare. Her deterioration had worsened since they last spoke. Her face was almost inhuman, with crevices sunk deeper than shipwrecks. "Are you okay?"

"I'm fine," she said.

Finn and his mother spent the next minute in rigid silence, the weight of their unspoken words hanging in the air between them, neither daring to utter the phrases they ought to. *I miss you. I love you.*

"I need your help," Finn said at last.

A skeptical expression crossed Emma-Lynn's face as her gaze shifted to the backpack slung over his shoulder. "Why can't *they* help you?"

Finn hadn't seen nor spoken to his mother since he left for college, a decision he knew wounded her, but one he had to make for his own well-being. He knew the "they" she spoke of referred to both his educators and the world outside her door.

"Because *they* don't understand what you do," he said. "I need to ask about the call."

Emma-Lynn's stance softened. She stepped to one side, allowing him to enter. "What happened?"

Finn walked past his mother and stepped into the living room, placing his backpack on the couch. "I'm writing a paper," he said, hoping to get the answers he sought without revealing his secret. "About Cthulhu's call, and its effect on people."

"A paper?" Emma-Lynn slammed the door. "You've come to dredge up the past over a paper?" Without waiting for his response, she strode by, disappearing into the kitchen.

Finn remained in the living room, giving her the opportunity to consider his request. It was the call of Cthulhu that had transformed her, after all. Cthulhu had taken her sanity, her life, and her husband.

Pictures of Finn's father still adorned the walls of her home, as they had during his childhood. The one thing he always loved about his mother was the way she preserved memories. Growing up, he would stare at each picture for hours, seeing himself in his father's big brown eyes, hoping to one day be as brave and courageous.

"The call is nothing," Emma-Lynn yelled. "There are fates worse than R'lyeh."

Finn joined her in the kitchen, taking a seat at the table. "Like what?"

"Waiting."

"What are you waiting for?"

Emma-Lynn sat next to Finn, slumping forward until her forehead dropped onto the tabletop. Her eyes were wide but motionless, peering at the wood grain like she was gazing through the lens of infinity.

Finn reached out, placing his hand on hers. "I didn't mean to upset you."

His mother remained silent, catatonic. These were the moments which fueled his desire to attend college and understand the inexplicable. What was Cthulhu's objective? How did he choose his victims?

The best documented recordings of the call were contained in the journal passages and online blog of Frances Smith, whom he studied at length. Driven by madness, Frances formed a cult following and sailed to R'lyeh, freeing Cthulhu from his bondage.

She had fallen in love with the deity from afar. But in the end, she was lured to her doom, dying with the false hope that she was called to meet her savior. Her blog posts have since been removed, but her journal became a revered text amongst cults. It also formed the basis of Professor Hartfield's lectures.

Like Finn's mother, Frances experienced the call, and lived somewhere between her dreams and reality, blurring the line between worlds, but neither Finn's mother nor Frances encountered a land of dreams as Finn had.

Finn wondered if he was experiencing the next phase in Cthulhu's plans, and if he would succumb to an untimely fate before avenging his father's memory.

"Does the name Nyar mean anything to you?" he asked.

"Nyarlathotep," she muttered through clenched teeth. "Why do you speak his name?"

"*Her* name—"

"This is no research paper." Emma-Lynn peeled her forehead off the table. "Nyarlathotep's name is not taught in *their* schools. He's a phantom, whispered about amongst cultists."

"I don't think we're talking about the same person."

"Has he visited you?" Emma-Lynn turned her gaze upon Finn, the fires of madness burning in her eyes as she awaited his answer.

"N . . . No," he choked.

Emma-Lynn seized his wrist, her yellow fingernails piercing his skin. "Don't lie to me."

Finn withdrew, recalling the tortured memories of his

childhood, when his mother's episodes would lead to the type of violent nightmares not even Cthulhu could conjure. He stood, freeing himself from her grasp, and ran for the door.

Emma-Lynn yelled after him. Her voice echoing off the walls, disjointed and frantic, as she tried to warn him about the unknown perils which lay ahead.

Finn tossed and turned in bed that night, unwilling to face the dreams which awaited his inevitable slumber. His mother's warning had dug itself into his skin, much like her nails, tearing up the sinew and burrowing into the bone where it nestled deep amongst his marrow.

Her psychotic episodes often lacked a basis in reality, but the way Nyar's name triggered her filled Finn with a sense of dread. Through a rational lens, the name she feared, Nyarlathotep, was too similar to be written off as a coincidence.

Finn fought to calm his labored breathing. To accept the inevitable. He was at the mercy of forces beyond his understanding. Acceptance of this truth was something his mother failed to adopt, and it had brought her nothing but trouble.

As panic set in, he imagined his apartment walls crumbling, revealing a haunting cosmic landscape beyond their veil, assuring him that reality was, in fact, a nightmare in and of itself. For what fate could be worse than being summoned to R'lyeh?

His heart pounded as he considered, now more than ever, that he was doomed to succumb to his visions, and to follow in his mother's footsteps to madness.

He pressed his eyes shut and fought the urge to scream. With deep breathing, he was able to lower his heart rate and slow the frantic thoughts which consumed his mind. "Whenever sleep takes me," he said aloud, "I will be at the mercy of my dreams."

THE SHADOW ENTITY

SLEEP DID NOT come for Emma-Lynn. Her gaze was fixed on the dream catchers dancing overhead, caught in the gusting winds from her shattered window panes. The night air carried with it an unseasonable chill, penetrating the thin sheet that covered her body and standing her hairs on end. There was but one being she feared these past twenty years, and his name was not Cthulhu.

From each corner of her home, an unpleasant thumping sounded. She squeezed her eyes shut. *A dream*, she told herself, refusing to believe another visitor beckoned at this hour. *Nothing to fear*.

The house rattled again, with a resonance that shook the foundation. At once, the winds ceased, replaced by an eerie stillness that sent shivers down Emma-Lynn's spine. Her dream catchers hung motionless above her head as she whispered through the tears.

"Go away."

As if such a trivial request could undo the actions set in motion all those years ago. She had hoped her memories of the shadow entity were but a nightmare, that her previous encounters with him were a delusional foray into the depths of madness.

Emma-Lynn rose from her bed, with terror welling inside her chest as she descended the rickety staircase and crescendoing as she pressed her face against the front door. Beyond the peephole lens lay nothing.

"Where are you, damnit?"

As Emma-Lynn turned her gaze away from the lens, tendrils of darkness snaked into her house. From every cracked window, through each air vent.

"Go away," she screamed. "You're not welcome here!"

Despite her pleas, the tendril persisted. They coiled around her, taunting her. Then they slithered together in the center of the home as a haunting figure—a slender man with no complexion; his skin was that of shadow, and the recesses of his eyes were filled with a dead light.

He stood tall, unphased by Emma-Lynn's pleas, and from the depths of his throat came a guttural and indifferent voice. "You knew this day would come."

Emma-Lynn knew at once, this was no nightmare. This visitor was quite real. Her heart beat faster as she gazed at the figure, seeing beyond any doubt it was the being who she feared most—Nyarlathotep.

"Stay away from my son!"

"You would rather watch the world burn?" Nyarlathotep asked. "Finn is the only person standing between the utter destruction of our realms. The time has come for him to fulfill his purpose, and for you to serve yours."

THE DREAMLANDS

WHAT BEGAN AS a dream had become a new reality, one which swallowed Finn whole. When sleep overtook him, he was once again transported to the otherworldly lands. This time, however, he was on the ground, lacking the grand perspective he held from the sky. Civilization was nowhere to be seen from this vantage, and the rift's location was obscured.

The purpose of these strange lands, and their connection to the ancient deity Cthulhu, remained shrouded in uncertainty. However, he feared such ambiguity would not last forever.

As he stumbled over the quartz-studded ground, his heart tensed, pulling at the muscle fibers in his throat, closing off his airway. The terrain grew dark, and the vibrant cosmic hues dimmed, creating an atmosphere of anticipation.

Now, more than ever, he understood and appreciated his mother's ongoing struggle to overcome her troubled dreaming. If there existed magical webs with which to catch these feelings of terror, wherein they could be disposed of, he would hang them over his bed as well.

Somehow his mind still thought of college, and the work which awaited him when he woke. As he trampled over the terrain, he worried his research paper would become a transcription of experience rather than a researched interpretation.

It was during this thought that a familiar figure materialized before him.

"Most dreamers must prove their worth to enter," Nyar said as her body solidified. Her right hand was raised as though she were offering a blessing. "You've bypassed the 700 steps to deep slumber, facing no judgement as those before you have."

"Those before me?"

"Indeed, and with my help, these lands will welcome you as no mere visitor, but a resident."

Finn shuddered. "Why did you bring me here?"

"You were led here by another; but I have shown you the truth which he hid from your eyes."

"The rift."

Nyar smiled. An affectionate smile with a dusting of fondness. "You possess latent abilities, unlike those of your peers. When you're here, you'll find they extend far beyond anything you thought possible."

"What is this place?"

"You're in the Dreamlands. A world between worlds, filled with mortals, beasts, and deities alike. Some call these lands home, while others are passersby, though only a gifted few are capable of entry."

"I was sure this was a vision, Cthulhu's call."

"Cthulhu led your mind here, but this place is no vision. The Dreamlands are quite real. When I first sensed your presence in the skies above, I knew I must intervene and enlighten you."

Finn couldn't ignore the tension brewing inside his stomach. "None of this aligns with what I've learned about Cthulhu. His only interest is luring mortals to R'lyeh. But the mention of *your* name sent my mother into hysterics; she chased me from her home."

"Listen to my words." The clouds above cast a foreboding shadow over Nyar's figure. "You saw what Cthulhu has in store. The rift is growing. It must be sealed before the nightmares can pass through."

Finn didn't wish to experience the pain she instilled, so he turned and ran. He knew not where he was headed, only that he must escape. He attempted to drown out Nyar's voice as he trampled over the ground, but her words persisted, reverberating throughout his mind.

They manifested inside of him, as if her whispers were his own thoughts. *You possess great power.*

"I do not."

You can peer through illusions, hear intentions, and channel cosmic energy.

"Nope."

You must take your rightful place.

Finn stopped; his palms pressed against his ears. "I'm not who you think I am."

Nyar re-materialized before him. She grabbed his shoulders and pried his eyes open with her will. Her voice no longer echoed in his mind. It assaulted him head on. "You are to become one with this world."

"I have school tomorrow, and a mother who needs help."

"You've never felt at peace, Finn. There's a fire burning in your heart. You wish to save the world."

Finn stared into Nyar's eyes, "How did you—"

"I know more than you can imagine. Finn, this is your chance. The nightmares won't stop here. They will use this world between worlds as a passage to every facet of existence. Everything you know, everyone you love, will fall."

"I can't battle an army of nightmares."

Nyar disregarded Finn's concerns, grazing her delicate hand upon his face before laying a peculiar amulet around his neck. "This charm will guide you in your dream-quest, and my father will protect your mortal coil in the waking world."

"Nyarlathotep?"

"My father's identity is not your concern."

Finn recoiled, feeling a surge of panic as the amulet hummed.

Nyar's hand transformed into a wisp of shadow and plunged through his chest, where it clung to his beating heart. Fire surged through his body as her eyes burned bright. It was a pain he could never have imagined.

"You have been fully assimilated, Finn. You are no longer a dreamer. You are a resident. If you feel this world has grown too dangerous," she said, sensing his terror. "Stomp your heel three times and wish to be brought home."

Finn dropped to his knees, clutching his chest. "Are you crazy?"

"When it comes to ritual, it's less about *what* you're doing and more about associating actions with a desired outcome. But take heed," she warned. "Your presence is required here." Nyar placed her hand on the amulet. "This charm will guide you, and only you, as a compass of light and resonance. Keep it close to your heart."

Before he could question Nyar about his dream-quest, a screech pierced the sky.

Nyar uttered the word, "Night-gaunt" and reached her hands into the air. "He knows you're here," she said, bringing her fingers to grasp the surrounding atmosphere. She pulled shadows from the sky itself, wrapping them around her body until she disappeared.

"Who knows that I'm here?" Finn rose to his feet, looking in every direction. "Hello."

Startled by another horrifying shriek, his gaze was drawn overhead. The Night-gaunt was circling like a bird of prey. Its body was unlike anything he had encountered. Long and gaunt, it resembled both man and bird. A starving, faceless, humanoid creature with bat-like wings sewn to its skeletal frame.

The wings beset an oily whale-like body which churned the pit of Finn's stomach, while menacing horns protruded from its head. Even from afar, the creature's immense paws were visible. They sported massive hooks, which were bared and ready to strike.

Finn had little choice but to follow Nyar's unusual instruction, kicking his heel into the ground and wishing to be home. He stomped again and again, sweat building on his brow. After a minute, he realized it was a useless act.

There's no way out.

Another screech pierced the sky. The creature made a swift directional change and pointed its razor-sharp hooks straight at Finn, diving through the air. In that panicked moment, he could hear his own heartbeat pounding in his ears.

Fueled by adrenaline, he stomped again. His heel crashed down. The impact reverberated through his body, and a hollow ring sounded as the ground gave way.

The Night-gaunt struck. Its hook penetrated Finn's chest and snagged on the amulet, suspending him over the sinkhole.

Finn grabbed at the creature's paw and ripped his amulet loose. Then he plummeted backwards through the sinkhole. His head collided with an unforgiving rock, sending a shockwave of pain through his body, which rendered his limbs paralyzed as darkness took hold.

RECLAIMING THE PAST

NYARLATHOTEP'S FORM GREW more defined. He towered over Emma-Lynn, no longer a mere shadow of the night, but solid enough to pass as a human. Even the enigmatic figure's garb, which had been the color of dusk, now burst with vibrant shades.

Emma-Lynn folded her arms, recognizing the implication. "You were projecting."

"It is my nature," Nyarlathotep said.

She was no stranger to the shadow entity's nature. Years prior, she bore witness to his shifting, and the memory of his ghoulish transformations remained as vivid now as they had been then. When Nyarlathotep expanded his presence, his primary form dematerialized.

"What kind of creep are you?" Emma-Lynn asked. "Manifesting as a girl to manipulate my son." She gritted her teeth, recollecting Finn's account of Nyar. "You disgust me."

A mischievous smirk played across Nyarlathotep's face. "There is no deception here. If your mortal religions can embrace the concept of a father, son, *and* holy Spirit, then I can be my own daughter."

"Stay away from my son, or you can be dead."

"You don't want to know what I can be," Nyarlathotep's gruff voice echoed through the home. His eyes ignited as shadows reached out from within. "I will not be threatened by the likes of you."

Emma-Lynn stood firm. "Where is Finn?"

"His mind is somewhere that his body is not." Nyarlathotep retracted his shadowy appendages, taking care to settle his nerves before continuing. "I warned you this day would come, that I spared your life for a reason. I only wish you had prepared the boy."

Emma-Lynn delivered a sharp slap to Nyarlathotep's face. "Prepared him for what?"

Nyarlathotep grabbed Emma-Lynn's wrist, twisting her arm until she fell to her knees before him. "Don't be so naïve. I had hoped there would be more time, but Finn's presence in the Dreamlands has not gone unnoticed."

"What are the Dreamlands?" Emma-Lynn asked, rising to face him once more.

Nyarlathotep was unaccustomed to such defiance, but as he required her aid, he provided greater disclosure than he wished. "The Dreamlands are a nexus between our worlds. They are in distress at the hands of a particular Great Old One, to which your son's fate is entwined."

"Cthulhu."

Nyarlathotep nodded. "Cthulhu is building an army. Creatures, the likes of which you cannot fathom, are being birthed in the skies above Mount Aran. If released, they need only to traverse the purple ridge of the Tanarians to reach the forbidden entryways into your world."

"What does Finn have to do with it?"

"You must recognize the implications of this breach," Nyar turned to leave, beckoning Emma-Lynn to follow him. "Immediate closure of the rift is imperative to safeguarding the Dreamlands, the waking world, and the equilibrium between realms."

Emma-Lynn's heart pounded. "I know who you are," she said, recollecting the dark tales she had learned of Nyarlathotep through whispers of the underground. "After you visited me, I studied you. You have no interest in aiding humanity."

"I know who *you* are," Nyarlathotep shot back, his eyes aflame. "Frances Smith."

Emma-Lynn fell to her knees. "It wasn't my fault!"

"All of this is your fault."

Long repressed memories swarmed Emma-Lynn's mind, plunging her back into the depths of the nightmare which unleashed hell on earth. "Cthulhu manipulated me."

Cthulhu seized control of Frances' escape vessel and drew it back to the shores of R'lyeh. Aboard the boat, alongside Frances, was her husband Donnie and her best friend Hazel.

Hazel fell first. Her heart exploded from Cthulhu's weaponized shriek, as though the sound had pierced her chest, collecting in her heart until it burst.

As Hazel's body crumpled to the deck, Cthulhu swept Frances and Donnie up in his tentacles, engulfing them in a putrid stench.

Armed with a fire axe, Frances locked eyes with Donnie, a bittersweet reminder that her heart would always belong to him.

Donnie smiled back, his eyes conveying a silent declaration of love, as he prepared his spear gun, taking aim at Cthulhu. With a forceful pull of the trigger, the spear soared through the air, piercing Cthulhu's right eye with a sickening thud.

Cthulhu's next shriek was one of agony as vile fluid gushed from the wound. But his grip on Frances and Donnie only tightened, his tentacles snaking around them like a boa constrictor suffocating its prey.

Frances mouthed the words 'I love you' to Donnie, feeling the intense pressure building up as darkness consumed her vision.

She regained consciousness on the deck of an unfamiliar boat, surrounded by darkness. Donnie was nowhere to be found. Inexplicable tendrils of darkness consumed the air, engulfing the fore-and-aft decks, as if guiding the voyage.

When Frances called out, the tendrils slithered together, forming the distinct humanoid shape of

Nyarlathotep. It was in that moment, separated from her husband, and at the mercy of an unknown entity, that Frances' mind shattered, and Emma-Lynn was born.

The long voyage home was filled with an eerie silence, broken only by Nyarlathotep's sparse and cryptic words. He introduced himself as a messenger of the Other Gods and revealed she had a pivotal role to play in their shared history. That one day, when the time was right, he would come for her.

Nyarlathotep snapped his shadowy fingers, jolting Emma-Lynn from her nightmarish recollection. "I know who you are, Frances Smith, and will call you by no other name. You don't deserve the luxury of hiding from the truth."

"Then Frances I shall be. For as long as I let you live."

Nyar glared back, his eyes exploding with dead light as he planted a warned straight into her mind. *If you interfere with my plans, I will expose you to the world and relish in the satisfaction of watching it dismantle you.*

Frances knew she had little recourse. Humanity had suffered for two decades because of her. That she wasn't in control of her mind would matter little to a society overrun by madness.

Should humankind discover Frances Smith was alive and well, living under an assumed name in her hometown of Boston, Massachusetts, retribution would be swift and deadly.

THE CAVERNS

INN WOKE TO the spatter of freezing water, his back flat against the unforgiving stone floor which had broken his fall. He rose to a seat and surveyed his surroundings: a cave chamber, from which branched a myriad of interconnected passages.

The passages bore an impenetrable darkness, which could harbor any manner of obstacle, making their exploration a hazard. He desired to remain where he was, but irreplaceable time had been lost, and he knew he must search for an escape.

Upon the cave walls, Finn spotted a canvas of deep claw marks, left by powerful creatures that called this place home. The light from his amulet cast eerie shadows over their grooves, heightening his senses and filling his mind with paranoia. He inhaled a dense and suffocating breath of subterranean air and tried to expel his fears.

Startled by another drip from a stalactite hanging overhead, he jumped. Wondering if it was a harmless droplet falling as it had for millennia, or the menacing salivate of a horrid cold-blooded creature suspended overhead, waiting for him to turn his back.

He crept along the nearest cave wall; hands brushing against the dirt as he tried to quell the terror brewing inside. His immediate concern was finding a way to the surface, as the hole he had fallen through was too high to be reached, and the walls leading up too steep and treacherous to scale.

Just as concerning, the ground beneath his feet was slick, and frequent gaps in the stone upon which he stood were a constant reminder that he could plunge to his death at any moment.

Finn caught his breath and crept into one of the chambers' many passages, praying he had chosen the correct one. The path narrowed, columns formed by the unrelenting drip and collection of mineral heavy water guarded the passage ahead like prison bars.

As he squeezed through the columns, strange noises greeted him, flopping and squelching.

How he longed for the comfort of his mother's concern, and the obnoxious behavior of his classmates, as he yielded to the facts: he was doomed, he did not possess the skills or wherewith-all to succeed.

After progressing a trivial distance, he surrendered himself to helplessness, resting his back against the nearest cave wall. But before he could settle in, he felt the disturbing sensation of tiny pincers teasing the back of his neck.

A sharp squeak sounded, accompanied by more terrible flopping noises.

He tore his body from the wall and spun around to see a small creature. It leapt onto his face, toppling him onto the ground.

Finn stood, disgusted by the trail of goop his attacker had left behind as it scampered away. The amulet around his neck summoned a bright glow, illuminating the strange creature. With its peculiar mix of bat and rodent features, it looked like a miniature demon, with a body so strangely proportioned that it turned Finn's stomach.

The creature's fur was clumped together, sticking to its greasy skin, as if covered in a slimy mucus akin to the secretions of a toad. Fearing poison, Finn wiped the viscous, salty ooze from his face and spat.

Then he investigated the wall from which the creature had descended. There was a small burrow, whereabouts he had lain his head, which originated from an unknown location and fed into this passage via the cave wall. Hope crossed Finn's mind. *Perhaps this burrow leads to the surface.* He held his amulet up to the opening and stuck his head inside.

The sound of flopping amplified, echoing through the burrow as Finn's presence stirred a frenzy. Shrieks rang out, and slime attacked his face. Soon, a swarm of peculiar creatures spewed forth as if through a birthing canal, forcing Finn from the opening.

Within a minute, there were a multitude of creatures writhing in goopy piles on the ground beneath the burrow, fluttering their membranous wings and calling out in a confusing symphony of what sounded like joy and terror.

Finn backed away, colliding with the opposing cave wall while the creatures continued to writhe and gather before him en masse. At last, a final grotesque form squeezed its way through the narrow burrow in the cave, and as it did, the frenzy stopped.

The other creatures formed an organized line behind the last to exit, as though they held some reverence for it. Then all of their eyes fixated on Finn, while their bodies paused, poised like trained dogs awaiting their leader's command. Some grew restless, shaking their bodies and spewing slime, while others quivered with anxious anticipation.

Finally, the lead creature took a step forward, nodding its head as if it wanted Finn to follow. The creature, and what could best be referred to as its pack, led a reluctant Finn through a labyrinth of tight walls until there came an opening.

Finn's amulet glowed again, emitting a disharmonious feeling that penetrated his ribs and pulled at his beating heart. The opening ahead fed into a massive chamber, wherein lay a horrifying cityscape of dimly lit cyclopean towers clustered in the center.

Such architecture was the work of advanced beings

27

capable of careful thought, planning, and cohesion. And the sheer size of the buildings, nay their entryways, was a testament to the grandiose size of their builders.

There was a sharp drop off where the passage ended, which gave Finn more reason to take pause, but the pack of strange creatures scurried down the slope without hesitation, leaving him with a choice: follow them into the oversized city or lose the only hope of finding a way out.

He disregarded the amulet's warning and followed, stumbling down the hillside. Once he reached the creatures, their pace intensified. They led him through a valley betwixt cliffs on a path winding up to the enormous stone structures ahead.

When they neared the city walls, the passage narrowed, and the silhouette of a large mound came into view, blocking the city gates which lay beyond. This mound was no passable hill, however. Rather, a nightmarish sentry slumped against the massive gates, which it must guard. The sentry, to Finn's relief, was overcome with slumber.

Finn fought to calm his nerves, quietly, without rousing the sentry. When to his shock, the lead bat-rodent creature showed no such caution. It hopped on top of the sentry, taunting it.

Several other creatures followed suit, scaling the sentry's torso and perching themselves upon its massive shoulders, where they pawed at the horizontal yellow fangs which stretched from one side of its grotesque, vertically oriented mouth to the other.

Finn waved his arms, attempting to recall the creatures before it was too late, but the sentry stirred. The ground beneath Finn's feet shook as the sentry sat upright, adjusting to its surroundings. It swiped at the little creatures as if they were flies buzzing around its head.

The longer the creatures taunted the sentry, the more aggravated it became, pounding and writhing until, at last, it stood, towering over twenty feet tall. It reared its bifurcated arms back and pointed its bony head straight up, salivate dripping from its fangs.

Finn expected a mighty roar, but the creature was mute. Perhaps the only advantage he had against such an insurmountable opponent was the fact that it couldn't rouse its allies with any immediacy.

Even alone, however, the sentry could devour them all with ease. The little creatures were aware of this as well, as evidenced by the flop and wail of their fleeing bodies.

With no remaining allies, Finn ran past the sentry and squeezed through the gates, not daring to look back. He sprinted through the twists and turns of the city by nothing more than the glow of his amulet, all the while hearing the crash of his pursuers' footsteps from behind.

At full speed, Finn remained mere inches ahead of the sentry's clawed digits, which sliced through the air like knives. He averted his course, ducking between the gap in a grand towers masonry.

A crippling blow followed, leveling several massive stones and leaving the tower in shambles. Finn continued to evade, passing through the stonework on the opposing side of the structure like a mouse through cracked molding.

More sentries, alerted by the destruction, rose from their slumber, silhouettes of their menacing forms towering amongst the distant stone walls.

Finn never broke pace, evading the monsters until he came upon a central tower of monumental proportions. Within, a grand staircase stretched to the top of the chamber. There he spotted one of the bat-rodent creatures, who was scaling the wall beside the stairway.

Finn closed in on the staircase, for he reasoned it must exit at the surface, away from these terrible beasts. The rise of each step was at least a yard, leaving little room for error. He ran at full speed and leapt onto the first step. Then he propelled himself up the massive staircase on all fours, using grooves and handholds in the rock to speed up the rises.

When he neared the top, where the stone walls gave way to dirt, his amulet's glow illuminated a sad truth. The passageway to the surface was blocked by a solid stone slab. Finn pushed hands against the stone, but it wouldn't budge.

He turned, realizing he had made a noisy ascent. At the base of the stairs stood a massive, fanged sentry, dialed in on his position. The sentry lunged up the steps, taking two at a time, its hungry eyes dying to feast upon raw flesh.

Another bat-rodent creature scurried past Finn and up the dirt wall, drawing his attention to a burrow situated just below the immovable stone slab.

Finn ran to the burrow and inserted himself, arms first, using his hands to pull his body inside. Working through the grimy hole was an arduous process, allowing the sentry ample time to bridge the gap between them with its lumbering gait.

The sentry grabbed Finn's legs and attempted to pull him from the burrow.

Finn dug his fingers into the mud, holding on with all his might. The ensuing tug of war yanked his legs from their sockets, but he held strong, pulling against the beast and kicking in every direction.

Massive claws dug into his skin, spurts of warm blood saturated his pant legs. He kicked harder, hoping to hit something sensitive. Though his initial attempts were fruitless, serving only to aggravate the sentry, his last kick struck its squishy, protruding eye.

There was a sickening pop followed by a splash of warm liquid which intermingled with the blood coating Finn's legs. The sentry loosened its grasp, and Finn pulled himself through, disappearing into the confines of the burrow.

Using all of his strength, he wormed his way through, doing what he could to avoid swallowing the mud which threatened to suffocate him. When the first rays of green light penetrated the burrow, Finn all but fainted from excitement, pulling with greater intensity to work past the last few inches of dirt.

Alas, he breached the surface and collapsed upon a forested landscape. Giant oaks stretched out overhead, their gnarled bark home to phosphorescence fungi—the source of the soothing green glow which had welcomed his escape.

Perhaps it was Finn's brush with death, but the entire woods seemed to radiate with a sense of enchantment that beckoned him to venture into their depths. *At last*, he thought, *somewhere peaceful.*

He forced his legs back into their sockets and pushed onward, but as he journeyed through the enchanted woods, the Night-gaunt swooped in from above. It crashed through the cluster of mighty oak trees, severing their branches as it plummeted to the ground.

THE CULT

RANCES FACED THE fresh air she disdained so, leading Nyarlathotep to Finn's apartment. The unpleasant breeze was like sandpaper against her damaged skin. Meanwhile, her fractured mind was still adjusting to the reclamation of her former identity and the tragic feelings it had awakened.

Had she not been under duress, and fearful for Finn's life, she never would have braved the world beyond her front door. But Nyarlathotep had set in motion events she could not overcome. She only hoped the shadow entity intended to protect Finn, as he claimed.

As Frances and Nyarlathotep neared the decrepit apartment complex, she wished she had fought harder to preserve her relationship with Finn. "His apartment is ground level," she whispered, observing Nyarlathotep's request for a stealthy approach.

Nyarlathotep clung to the shadows, taking a moment to scold Frances as he circled the building. "If we're lucky, your resistance won't have cost Finn his life."

The shadow entity shared but one detail with Frances during their trek—that Finn's assimilation with the Dreamlands rendered him unable to rouse, leaving his body vulnerable to attack.

Therefore, it was imperative they take possession of his physical form, lest he fall into the wrong hands. That much made sense to Frances, but the finer details of Finn's dream-quest remained a mystery.

Frances didn't understand why Finn had to be involved at all. "Who ordered you to do this?" she asked. "You're a messenger of the other gods."

"I work for a blind idiot," Nyarlathotep smirked, and in nature befitting his character jested, "who among us does not?"

"Do you mean Az—"

"I suggest you let sleeping dogs lie."

Frances bit her tongue and pointed to an exterior hall which led to a row of ground level studios. "Turn right," she said. "He's in apartment 115."

Nyarlathotep took the lead and turned the corner. "Stop," he ordered, throwing his fist in the air.

Frances peered past his fist. The door to 115 had been removed. She charged down the hall and hurried into Finn's apartment.

Inside, she found no evidence of a struggle. Everything was where it should have been, except for Finn. His coat was hung on its rack, and his bed was made to look as if no one had been in it.

"Finn's been taken," she screamed.

Nyarlathotep entered behind her, his eyes aflame with dead light. "Finn mustn't be harmed during his dream-quest."

"How long until he wakes up?"

"There is a temporal distortion between the Dreamlands and the waking world."

Frances threw her hands in the air. "Meaning what?"

"Finn's journey could last days, weeks, or months in the Dreamlands, which could mean seconds, minutes, or hours in the waking world, or vice versa. But his journey *will* end abruptly if his body falls to the wrong people."

Frances sprinted outside, headed in the opposite direction from which they came. Nyarlathotep hurried after her, his footsteps gliding over the cracked walkway that connected the apartments to the parking lot.

Past the lot, nestled within the adjoining woods,

33

Frances spotted a group of cloaked men moving between the trees. They were carrying what looked like an ornate, lidless coffin.

She turned to Nyarlathotep. "Finn must be inside."

"Lower your voice," he demanded. "This is a fortunate turn of events."

"Fortunate?"

The sight of Finn being paraded around in a coffin left Frances reeling. She opened her mouth to protest, but Nyarlathotep silenced her with nothing more than a gesture, weaving his fingers in the air as if he had threaded a shadow through her lips; her words caught in her throat, and her mouth sealed shut, allowing only the faintest whimper to escape.

"Observe, they are treating Finn with reverence," Nyarlathotep loosed the seal on her lips. "We mustn't instigate a battle when the fate of our worlds hangs in the balance. These men do not pose an immediate threat."

"Those men are Cthulhu cultists."

"We will follow them," Nyarlathotep assured. "Perhaps they can be of use."

"Where do your allegiances lie?" Frances felt a profound sense of unease wash over her as she grappled with the uncertainty surrounding Finn's fate. "Are you in bed with Cthulhu, with his followers?"

Nyarlathotep was swift to deny her assertion. "A messenger of the other gods, working with the Cthulhu Cult?" he laughed. "Mortals, ignorant of their own beliefs and actions, who stumble through life aimlessly."

"I wouldn't put it past you."

"If it weren't by divine order, I would never have saved, nor associated with the fool who awakened Cthulhu, let alone work for Cthulhu's followers. Nevertheless, they have learned of Finn's significance. We must ascertain their goals, lean on their resources, and fight back only if it is in the best interest of our worlds."

THE ENCHANTED WOODS

FINN INVESTIGATED THE lifeless Night-gaunt. Felled branches surrounded the creature, which lay motionless among a cluster of phosphorescent fungi where it crash landed. Rather than flee, however, Finn found himself enamored with the peculiar creature.

He picked a sturdy branch from the ground, about the heft of a baseball bat, and took an uncertain step closer. His wounded legs shook with a mixture of fear and exhaustion as he crouched to get a more comprehensive look.

The Night-gaunt's blubbery flesh was aglow amidst the fungi. Its head lacked a face and was beset by only horns. There were no ears, eyes, nor mouth or nose, not a single orifice. *How did you track me*, he wondered, *and what do you want with me?*

More unsettling than the Night-gaunt's lack of sensory organs was its humanoid appearance, its limbs both familiar and alien at the same time. And those disgusting membranous wings did not belong upon the protruding vertebrae to which they were attached.

Finn prodded the Night-gaunt with his branch, unsure if it were alive or dead until the creature shuddered, standing erect with such intensity that he fell backwards.

The Night-gaunt's grotesque and faceless head studied him from above, moving with the agility of a bird of prey as it darted in quick, jerking motions.

Finn lay still, quelling his breath as he tightened his grip on the branch. His body was motionless, except for his heart, which throbbed in his chest.

Using its massive, hooked paw, the Night-gaunt clutched Finn's amulet, tearing it from his neck with a piercing screech. Then it turned and sprinted across the forest at the speed of an ostrich, carving a path through the dense foliage.

Finn used his branch to pull himself off the ground. He attempted to chase the Night-gaunt, but his injured legs would only carry him so fast. Soon, the thick canopy of twisted oak and leaves blotted out the creature, leaving him alone in the woods.

Noises from unidentified creatures echoed in his ears. Anxiety crept into his chest. The pain in his legs intensified. He wouldn't make it far without rest, but every second spent here brought him closer to madness.

Using the elephant leaves of a nearby plant, Finn tended to his wounds. The plant's sturdy leaves served as bandages to slow the blood loss, and the vicious secretion from their thick stems help seal the leaves in place.

Then, using the mossy roots of a tree as a makeshift pillow, he let his fatigue take over. But no sooner than he closed his eyes, a bat-rodent creature scurried past.

Finn no longer trusted the creatures, though there may be a source of food or water nearby which this one sought. Essentials he didn't expect to need here, and yet, he knew he required sustenance if he were to continue his journey.

His focus narrowed as he exerted every ounce of remaining energy to follow the elusive creature. His bloodied legs pounded the ground with surprising speed. *This pain*, he thought as his legs throbbed from the impact, *might it be real?*

The creature looked back at Finn, noticing his inability to maintain pace. Its beady eyes glinted with a devious invitation to keep following. It was a look which gave Finn pause, considering his previous encounter, but he couldn't risk losing a knowledgeable guide.

Finn nodded to the creature, "if you understand English, I need water."

Without a moment's hesitation, the bat-rodent creature let off an "eeeekrh," then scurried along its path, guiding Finn deeper into the twisted woods.

Through winding and densely forested paths, Finn followed, stepping over felled trees whose bark shone like fragmented crystal and crouching under strands of silver that danced like moss in the breeze.

Before long, he found himself in a clearing, surrounded by a circular formation of large, alien plant life. In the center of the clearing there stood an enormous tree, and hanging from a twisted branch was his amulet.

"Is this where the Night-gaunt lives?" Finn crouched beside the rodent. "You found my amulet," he said, his voice breaking as he stared at the hideous creature. "You've been following my dream-quest."

The creature responded by flapping its wings, ejecting a gelatinous goop that flew in all directions.

"Thank you," Finn said, placing his hand on the creature. "At least someone is looking out for me."

THE CATHEDRAL

RANCES AND NYARLATHOTEP tracked the cultists procession for miles. When in the distance a spire peeked out over the treetops, Frances knew where they were headed. It was the same location where the Cthulhu Cult had ensnared her twenty years prior: their aging gothic cathedral, a hub for vile, ritualistic gatherings.

Standing in the shadow of the ominous masonry, she froze, trembling with fear as echoes of her past encounters collided with the reality of her present. Memories of the strange eldritch symbols the cult had painted upon her naked flesh abounded. She could still hear the voices of the fractured organization's members as they discussed her fate.

Her son was now forced to endure the same fate which had befallen her, beholden to the Cthulhu Cult, his mind trapped in a journey set to alter the course of human history.

Frances watched as the cultists hefted the ornate coffin, with Finn's lifeless body still in it, up the grand cathedral steps, and carried him through the colossal entryway doors. Doors which, in recent years, had been adorned with ornate tentacles, indicative of a counter culture organization which no longer felt compelled to exist in the shadows.

"We will protect your son," Nyarlathotep assured, his shadowy hand resting on Frances' shoulder in an unusual gesture of warmth and empathy.

Frances placed her hand on top of his. "Let's take these sons of bitches down."

Nyarlathotep withdrew his hand, settling into a more fitting defiance. "We must understand their intentions. The cult is following Cthulhu's command. It would behoove us to understand what our enemies have in store, and how we may use them to our advantage."

"I understand them fine," Frances said. "My mission is to save Finn."

"In this, we are aligned."

"Then we do whatever it takes to get him back."

"It takes planning."

Nyarlathotep led Frances through the foliage, coming to a stop alongside the cathedral. "Stick to the shadows," he instructed. "Deny your base instinct to charge in headfirst and live to fight with every tool in your arsenal."

"I have no tools."

"What do you know of this cult?"

"The cultists are often at odds with one another," Frances said, recalling her previous encounters with them. "They are fools, drawn in by the cult's power. They have no regard for Finn's safety."

"Yet, they have no need for his death."

"This building is used for rituals." Frances' heart beat faster as she fought to keep her anxieties at bay. "The cultists gather here for sacrifices and—"

"To commune with deities and realms beyond the reach of mortal comprehension," Nyarlathotep said. "The cultists have visited the Dreamlands, and Finn possesses a connection that they wish to exploit."

Frances gave a hesitant nod. "If things go south, Finn is your priority."

Trusting Nyarlathotep was difficult for her. While there were no stories of Nyarlathotep inflicting direct harm upon a mortal, the entity was no fan of hers. Yet, he seemed to harbor no ill-will towards Finn.

So, with Nyarlathotep's assurance, Frances

approached the side entrance of the cathedral. She opened the door, releasing a pungent and oppressive scent which assaulted her senses. Then swallowed her fears and beckoned for Nyarlathotep to follow.

Together, they slunk through the cathedral's dark recesses. Progressing under the shimmer of cobwebs, they made their way through the smaller service rooms and corridors encircling the grand halls until, at last, they emerged in the nave, a vast space that exuded an overwhelming sense of verticality.

An imposing statue of Cthulhu had been erected in the center of the chancel. Additionally, the cult's collection of medieval weaponry, which had spanned a single wall twenty years prior, now covered every wall of the interior. Blood-stained artifacts, old and new, served as a haunting reminder of the terrors that endured within this building.

As Frances and Nyarlathotep peered out from behind the wooden pews, the cultists moved Finn's body from the ornate coffin to a raised platform positioned on the left of the chancel. There was a second, unoccupied raised platform on the right side.

The cultists chattered excitedly amongst themselves, their voices rising and falling in a symphony of anticipation, until they were joined by an elder, whose hunched posture and slow, weary steps hinted at lifetime's passage.

Silence washed over the cultists as they awaited their elder's instruction, and the old man wasted no time in communicating their next steps. Before long, the platform on the rightmost side of the chancel was occupied by a dedicated volunteer, who was ready to offer himself as Finn's spiritual guide within the Dreamlands.

Frances looked at Nyarlathotep. "What do they mean, spiritual guide?"

Nyarlathotep, with his eyes locked on the brewing ritual, replied, "they are sending one of their own into the Dreamlands to engage with Finn, perhaps to win his favor and allegiance."

"Or kill him."

Nyarlathotep shook his head. "Their intentions are unclear, but they have no desire to bring harm to Finn. They may be of use yet."

Frances watched the cultists shuffling about the chancel, their movements synchronized and purposeful as they formed a circle which encompassed both raised platforms. Once in position, the elder cultist handed out torches, which, as lit, cast an eerie glow on the yellowing, brittle sheets of papyrus he distributed next.

The script laden papyrus was passed around in counterclockwise formation, which Nyarlathotep explained was significant to this mystical practice, setting the stage for these practitioners to disrupt and reverse the natural order of things.

The atmosphere became an unnerving play of synchronized shadow and strange chants as the cultists raised their torches high. Even with the grand entry doors closed, a powerful gust of wind found its way into the great hall, causing smoke to rise and gather in swirling clouds beneath the towering cathedral arches.

Defying Nyarlathotep's will, Frances stood from behind the pews, facing several cultists who broke their rank to confront her. "Stop the ritual!"

The chanting continued while those cultists stood as guardians, preventing her from reaching the chancel until the ritual was complete.

Meanwhile, Nyarlathotep remained in hiding, leaving Frances alone. With determination in her eyes, she charged the chancel, forcing the guardians to hold her in place.

"Do you have any idea who I am?" she asked.

The men's faces remained stoic beneath their hooded cloaks, their grasp on her firm. Uncertain of her next move, Frances clung to the hope that her notoriety would captivate them. For history knew of her only as the person who released Cthulhu.

"You must know of Frances Smith."

The cultists looked at one another, answering in unison. "We do."

"She did not perish in R'lyeh." Frances saw her opening, a chance to convince the cultists that she had returned to lead them. "I am Frances Smith," she declared. "The woman who awakened Cthulhu. I require Finn's body and your unwavering allegiance."

The Cultist

INN REACHED OUT to claim his amulet from the tree branch where it hung, though he couldn't help noticing a peculiar spectacle unfold. The amulet flickered, as a projection might, and his hand recoiled from the resulting static.

Taking a step back, he noticed his creature companion had disappeared, and the forest's glow had waned. Thoughts were whispered to him by the winds, unveiling subtle inconsistencies in the atmosphere.

A flash of color where one oughtn't be, static reverberations alive in the air, then waves of tension.

The lone tree loomed over Finn as if it were extending its hand; a spindly wooden finger reaching out with wicked temptation as the amulet dangled from it.

Before he could grasp the amulet, a cyclone of air engulfed him, shifting his orientation. Within the whirlwind, a cloaked man appeared, surrounded by a crimson haze, compelling Finn in his native tongue to halt and heed a message.

Finn turned back to the tree and grabbed the amulet, intending to flee from the haunting vision. As he did, however, darkness engulfed the forest. The last remnants of glowing foliage faded away. Leaves clustered together to obstruct the moonlight from filtering through.

The canopy overhead came alive as hundreds of beady eyes blinked open in unison, their glassy surfaces reflecting the amulet's glow.

The amulet flickered again, losing its weight and heft before vanishing from Finn's hand. *This truly is a land of deception*, he thought, before shouting, "you never had the amulet, you little bastards."

A multitude of disgusting creatures leapt from the trees in response.

Their feet clung to his body, vying for dominance. Sharp claws tore into his skin, leaving trails of blood in their wake. The makeshift bandages on his legs were ripped off as his knees collided with the ground, crushing two of his attackers' skulls.

The sickly sound of their fragile bones shattering beneath him was accompanied by a nauseating spew of slime. Finn choked on bile as he succumbed to the weight of the descending creatures. They forced him to the ground and piled on, making it impossible to breathe as they denied his lungs the room to expand.

Finn surrendered to the onslaught, destined to meet a torturous demise under the relentless attack of these manipulative creatures. He pressed his eyes shut, wondering if his inevitable demise would impact his body in the waking world. But as he awaited death's embrace, something extraordinary happened.

A surge of energy burst forth, igniting the mountain of bat-rodent attackers. Their high-pitched screams echoed through the air as they were flung into the distance.

The mound of creatures, once vying for control over him, disintegrated into a chaotic jumble of quivering masses; their bodies strewn about the woods. Gasping for breath, Finn wiped their goopy blood from his eyes, desperate to see where the blast had originated.

It was the mysterious cloaked man. A charm dangled from the man's neck, reminiscent of Finn's lost amulet, but featuring a rectangular frame encasing a glass sphere. Finn could tell that the blast had been channeled through this sphere by the smoke wafting from its surface.

"Never trust a Zoog," the cloaked man warned, his

voice muffled by the dense smoke that hung in the air. He kicked aside the charred body of a bat-rodent creature and offered his hand. "I know of your quest, my brother, and I promise you. Your trust is best placed in my guidance."

THE FLAIL

T HE CTHULHU CULT was none too impressed with Frances' disruption, and as she stood her ground amongst their torch wielding ranks, she knew she was too late to halt the ritual. Atop the rightmost podium, the young cultist's eyes had glassed over. His mind was detached from his body, no doubt communing to the Dreamlands to ensnare her son.

With their ritual complete, the cultists' chanting ceased, and their eyes fell upon Frances in unison, their torches pointed in her direction as the elder spoke.

"We are aware of your identity, Frances Smith, and were content to leave you to your madness. But your actions have shown us you are unwilling to accept what must be done."

Frances choked on her words, swallowing the bile that wretched up her throat. "If you know who I am, then you know Finn is my son. I won't leave without him."

The surrounding air grew tense, filled with fire, smoke, and the discontent of the cultists. They progressed in unison, marching like a choreographed herd in her direction. Heat wafted over her face from the torches as they drew near.

Frances backed up, feeling droplets of sweat bead upon her forehead as she debated fleeing. The cultists didn't care who she was or what she had done for their cause. Their only concern was her son, taking control of his body, and leading his mind to serve their will, just as Nyarlathotep wanted for himself.

She looked back at the pews. *Where has that shadowy deceiver gone?*

A wisp of shadow graced the ear of a cultist who was progressing in Frances' direction. The cultist froze, subdued by a subtle whisper, and turned to his companions in rage.

"You wish to rouse the boy," he said, setting his torch to his associate's garments.

Shadows danced between the congregation, whispering commands and accusations, which were followed by shoves, punches, and discontent amongst their ranks.

Frances breathed a sigh of relief, believing at last that Nyarlathotep intended to protect Finn. She seized upon the chaos, racing to the nearest wall of medieval weaponry with several cultists on her tail.

Most weapons on display were beyond her ability to wield, but she spotted a lightweight option. Without breaking stride, she leapt and snatched a flail from its hook, then turned to face her pursuers.

The cultists hung back, arming themselves with an array of weaponry. Two turned their attention to Frances, while the others swiped at the air, hoping to quell the whispering shadows which darted amongst them.

Of the cultists who faced Frances, one wielded a sword of thirty inches, while the other retrieved a halberd of six feet. The ranged attack potential of the latter was enough to disembowel Frances while invalidating her flail's usefulness.

She reared back, as if to swing a baseball bat, and released her flail at the halberd wielding cultist. The flail spun through the air, catching the cultist by the throat. His larynx was crushed by the impact as his eyes burst from their sockets. He tried to scream, but the vague whisper was drowned out by the blood pouring from his mouth.

Frances was left weaponless. But a wisp of shadow caught the sword wielding cultist's ear, hissing an unsettling command into his mind. The cultist stopped his charge just before reaching Frances, pointed his head at the ceiling, and raised the sword.

Frances watched in horror as the man turned the sword on himself, inserting it into his mouth. He must have retained some control, as his arms fought to keep the blade at bay, but his struggles were in vain.

Another whisper deepened the shadow entity's hold. The cultist plunged the blade deep into his throat. Blood spilled out over his lips, but he kept pushing until the blade popped through the back of his neck, severing his spinal cord and dropping him to the floor.

Frances retrieved her flail. The weapon was lodged deep within the first cultist's throat, lifting his head off the ground before the spiked ball dislodged itself with a nauseating squelch.

She clutched the flail tight, preparing for battle, but as she gazed upon the chancel, she faced a horrific scene. Cloaked bodies impaled and burned, dead and dying in heaps . . . only one man was left unharmed.

The cultist on the rightmost platform, her son's so-called spiritual guide. Frances tightened her grip on the flail and progressed on the platform, resolute in killing him.

Nyarlathotep re-materialized in front of Frances. "Stop!"

"Out of my way."

"No, this man will be of use to Finn. We must spare him."

Frances surveyed the pile of blood-stained cloaks and splayed bodies surrounding them. "If you think you can stop me from protecting my son," she said, side-stepping Nyarlathotep. "You don't understand the depth of will I've developed."

"If you want Finn to succeed, this man must live."

"You lie."

"Finn does not know how to navigate the Dreamlands, but this man does."

Frances dropped her flail, where it landed upon a cultist's severed head. "You killed them these men on your own," she said. "There are no limits to your earthly abilities, yet you claim to need me. Why?"

A New Path

INN'S CLOAKED VISITOR refused to provide his name but identified himself as a member of the Cthulhu Cult, a blatant admission which tugged at Finn's doubts and insecurities. He grew up fearing cults, yet this cultist had done nothing but help.

Since obliterating the strange looking Zoog creatures, the cultist continued his good will by setting up camp, collecting liquid filled gourds of moon-wine from the hollow of the Zoogs' home tree, tending to Finn's wounds, and building a fire.

This cultist was no stranger to the Dreamlands, gathering supplies and edible plants from the forest to sustain their journey. He was able to identify the monstrous creatures from the subterranean cyclopean city as well. They were known as Gugs.

Many of the creatures afoot held unassuming names, and deception was at the forefront of the cultist's teachings. The cultist also confirmed something Finn had feared since suffering his first painful attack—for him, death bore an unavoidable consequence.

Despite these lands being host to beings from different realms and states, their encounters, and interactions occurred at varying levels. The cultist had communed here through a ritual, which was akin to dreaming. If a dreamer meets their demise in the Dreamlands, their consciousness transfers back to their unscathed physical form.

The native Dreamlandians had no form beyond the

Dreamlands. If killed, they would not only vanish from the Dreamlands, but from the fabric of reality itself. However, the longer they persisted, the more powerful they became, and with no natural or set expiration, some were essentially immortal, surviving for thousands of years while their weaker counterparts perished.

Finn's was a special and unfortunate case. According to the cultist, his assimilation was performed by a malign deity who granted him the status of resident at the behest of a festering evil.

This unique situation allowed Finn to maximize his potential as a Dreamlandian might, but should he be killed, his physical body would be left an empty shell, with a mind forever relinquished to the awful voids outside the ordered universe where gnaws the daemon-sultan Azathoth—a mindless, blind, and tenebrous deity.

After hearing of his potential fate, Finn fixated on the fire, his mouth agape in silent astonishment. The cultist, sensing Finn's alarm, steered the conversation back to the Zoogs, noting how they had grown increasingly hostile throughout the years after much warring with the cats.

"Cats?" Finn asked, his presence restored by the absurdity.

The cultist nodded. "It's not so strange here," he said. "You needn't fear the cats, either. They are benevolent and wise, though fierce. The Zoogs are defeated with ease, and the Gugs are trapped beneath the stone doorway you spoke of earlier. The Cthulhu Cult values you, Finn. We will not allow you to fall victim to Azathoth."

"Why do you refer to your organization as a cult?" Finn asked, his lips loosened by the moon-wine and his fears quelled by the cultist's confidence. "Other people call you cultists, but I would expect you to refer to yourselves in higher regard."

"What we call ourselves is of little importance."

"So, like the Divine Brotherhood of the Squid, or the Order of the Tentacle."

"The world recognizes the name Cthulhu Cult, and they know us as cultists. Our organization has been a venerable force since before my birth and will continue to inspire long after my death. Tell me, if you were so revered, would you advertise by another name?"

Finn stared into the rhythmic dance of flame, contemplating the cultist's words. This nameless man spoke with wisdom, and after a short time, had provided both protection and invaluable guidance on how to survive within the Dreamlands.

"Perhaps the Cthulhu Cult is not as sinister as I was led to believe."

"We are not the sinister ones."

Finn knew the cultist was referring to Nyar as the sinister one, someone whom Finn had trusted, who abandoned him in the Dreamlands with no guidance. The cultist had described Nyar as a malign deity.

"What does your cult want with me?" Finn asked.

"We've taken possession of your earthly body," the cultist said, "but there will be others seeking to apprehend you in this world and in the waking one."

"Nyar told me that her father would protect my waking body. She gifted me the amulet I'm seek . . . " Finn paused, wondering if he was right to place his faith in this cultist, for he had not yet divulged the details of his dream-quest.

"Nyar has no father."

"She does. His name is Nyarlathotep, I suspect."

"What I mean to say is," the cultist clarified. "Nyarlathotep is the only entity. Nyar is one of a million different forms which he takes."

Startled by the revelation, Finn thought back to his interactions with Nyar and his introduction to the Dreamlands. "Why lie about his identity?" he asked. "I didn't know either of them. There was no reason to lie."

"There was," the cultist chuckled, a momentary break in his otherwise serious demeanor. "Is a young man more likely to sacrifice himself for an attractive young woman or a shadowy entity who looks like evil incarnate?"

"A young woman, I suppose . . . I would have helped either way."

"Nyarlathotep wanted to be sure, to play every conceivable angle. That's what he does. His entire presence is a deception. Tell me, what does he want you to do?"

Finn couldn't help feeling betrayed, yet still hesitant. "What do *you* want me to do?"

"Nothing," the cultist said. "I am here to provide you with safe passage to Celephaïs. The Great One has spoken to us, and we must deliver you to King Kuranes."

"The Great One. Cthulhu." Finn tried to contain his disbelief. "He knows who I am? What the hell does Cthulhu want from me?"

"I only know that Celephaïs is where you are needed."

"Cthulhu said this?" Finn asked. "The tentacled deity who lures people to their doom."

"Has Cthulhu left R'lyeh and taken control of our world?" The cultist continued without waiting for a reply. "To pave the way for humanity's next leap, there will be a culling of the feebleminded. Those resilient to control will succeed."

"How many will die?"

"Without the perspective of timelessness, I don't expect you to understand Cthulhu's means, but trust he is working towards a greater world."

Finn tried to resolve the cultist's words. "But Nyar . . . Nyarlathotep, cares for people."

"Nyarlathotep cares only for himself," the cultist exhaled, like a frustrated parent trying to explain the intricacies of their job to a child. "Cthulhu's motivations are beyond your comprehension. Sacrifice is necessary, but he values cosmic order. His imprisonment on R'lyeh was unwarranted. Journey with me, Finn. I trust you will come to understand the important mission which awaits you in the city of Celephaïs."

THRAN

AS THE SUN rose the next morning, Finn and the cultist embarked on a journey to Celephaïs. Nyarlathotep's dream-quest and the impending rift continued to weigh on Finn's thoughts, as did his decision to aid in Cthulhu's agenda. Truth be told, he trusted in neither Cthulhu nor Nyarlathotep, but the cultist was someone whom he placed faith in.

Without the amulet, he required someone trustworthy. Exploring the Dreamlands alongside a knowledgeable guide would grant him the opportunity to uncover the rift's location without fearing death. He couldn't be sure if the cultist would help him close the rift when the time came, but the cultist's fond descriptions of Celephaïs made Finn hopeful.

The cultist spoke of Celephaïs as a place where time had no influence, where everything remained fresh and unspoiled. He seemed a reasonable man who would not wish to unleash madness upon Celephaïs' inhabitants, nor any Dreamlandian.

"King Kuranes was a dreamer of great power," the cultist explained as he led the way through a vast field. "Celephaïs is a city of his mind's creation. He dreamed it into being."

"How is that possible?"

"Some among us are gifted. The king is an anomaly, like yourself, in that he is an honorary resident of the Dreamlands."

Finn struggled to keep pace, using a scavenged branch as a crutch to aid his wounded legs in pressing onward as he sputtered out his words. "How was the king assimilated?"

"Kuranes once lived in the English countryside of the waking world," the cultist said. "But such a dreamer he was that when his physical body succumbed to the tides and washed up upon the shores of Innsmouth, his mind remained anchored in the Dreamlands."

Over countless hills of varying terrain, the cultist regaled Finn with tales of the great King Kuranes and the Dreamlands, providing guidance sprinkled with history, and pointing out landmarks along the way.

While Finn appreciated the stories, he found that many were peppered with warnings about trusting malign deities, such as Nyarlathotep.

"What did the shadow entity request of you?" the cultist asked, assessing the impact of his latest cautionary tale.

Finn gripped his crutch as he stumbled over the ground, attempting to match the cultist whose speed and intensity increased each time he spoke of Nyarlathotep. "I was only shown a vision."

"What were you shown?

"Something terrible," Finn said, choosing to remain vague. "Above a mountain."

"Finn," the cultist said, his frustration clear, "there are countless mountains in the Dreamlands." He trampled down the hill, leading to a vast expanse of fields. "We're not just following the path of *a* river."

"We're not?"

"No, we're following the singing river Oukranos. It's a willow-fringed river beside a golden field."

"So?"

"Describe the mountain to me. What was the terrain like? The flora and fauna. Were there bodies of water nearby which I could use as a point of reference?"

"It doesn't matter. You're leading me to Celephaïs to meet the king."

"Of course it matters," the cultist said, his voice filled with conviction as he came to a sudden halt. "Your quest may run counter to the Great One's mission, undermining our objectives. Tell me, were there any gingko trees in your vision? Could it have been the peaks of Mount Aran you saw, beside Celephaïs?"

Finn stopped to catch his breath, then shrugged. "Could have been."

Taking a moment to absorb his surroundings, Finn wished he were without the cultist or the burden of a quest. The colors of a thousand flowers painted the ground beneath his feet, while a blessed haze kissed them each with dew. The river Oukranos itself was a wonder, alive with iridescent fish that glided through its clear waters like shimmering gemstones.

"Focus," the cultist said. "We must reach Thran by nightfall and charter a ship to Celephaïs."

The cultist took off, his hurried footsteps flattening a trail through the tall flowers ahead. Finn hurried after, and they didn't pause again until midday, taking a moment to observe the jasper terraces of Kiran.

Finn used the opportunity to drink from the river. Then, after scrounging edible fungi to sustain their trek, they continued without another break until nightfall. It was then that the cultist reached a grassy rise and came to a sudden halt.

"Where is it?"

"Where is what?" Finn asked, gasping for breath as he fought to remain upright.

"The thousand gilded spires of Thran, the alabaster walls, everything!"

Beyond the cultist, Finn spotted a flicker in the air just ahead of their position. The shimmer was barely noticeable, but it reminded him of the strange inconsistencies he had encountered while seizing the Zoogs' false amulet.

"It's an illusion," Finn said. "Someone doesn't want us here."

He approached the flicker, caressing the surrounding air until he felt a tingle course through his body. Then a soft, melodic hum filled the air.

"Why are you waving your hands like a madman?" the cultist asked.

Finn paid no mind to the rudeness; he knew something was near. A hole in the illusion. Alas, vindication came when his fingers struck the proper alignment and slid into the flickering ends of what could only be described as living fabric.

His hands delved deep into the fabric, and as he pulled at them, the hum intensified, filling the surrounding air with crackles and pops. Flickering lights danced before his eyes as he beheld a grand city beyond the illusory cloak.

Ahead, he saw Thran's gates opened onto the Oukranos river, revealing grand wharves made of polished marble and ancient walls, of a construction that defied explanation, towering over the swaying galleons at anchor.

Finn found himself entranced by the beauty, but as he lingered, his hands bound with the fabric, making it difficult for him to break away. He called on the cultist to pass through, holding the fabric open like a tent flap, then followed with haste, slipping inside and pulling his fingers free from their bind. As the fabric released its hold on him, he watched the invisible cloak seal itself.

"Come on," the cultist called back. "Thran awaits."

Finn hurried along, following the cultist to the wharves. Fragrant cedar and calamander filled the air as they drew nearer to the ships. They passed by several mighty galleons with anticipation but found no sailors amongst them.

"Lousy drunkards." The cultist pointed to a grand stairway ahead. "We must search the taverns."

They progressed past another gate and ascended Thran's steps, an arduous journey to undertake on wounded legs, but Finn's crutch carried him to the city above.

The streets were lined with vibrant bazaars, boasting a variety of wares, yet no merchants tended them. The entire city appeared to be missing, abandoned as though its residents had disappeared.

"Maybe they're sleeping," Finn said.

"Not likely." The cultist weaved through the barren moonlit streets, motioning for Finn to follow. "Thran's steps are never left unguarded. Something is wrong here." The cultist edged back down to the river and burst into a sea tavern. "All galleon captains identify yourselves."

Finn stumbled in after the cultist to find a sparsely occupied bar.

There was a large man in a tricorn hat sitting in front of the bar, from which came a solitary "aye." The captain's head was surrounded by drifting smoke, its silver wisps mingling with the unruly grey hairs that stuck out from his hat.

The cultist approached the captain, propping an aggressive elbow on the bar and drawing attention to the satchel hidden within his cloak. "We require passage to Celephaïs."

Through another cloud of smoke, the captain announced, "it's fallen."

"Celephaïs, the deathless city." The cultist snatched the captain's pipe, his eyes narrowing with suspicion. "What do you mean, fallen?"

The captain stood, his imposing figure looming over the bar, and retrieved his pipe from the cultist's hand. "I mean, it's fallen," he said, with a hint of sorrow in his voice. "Nobody sails to Celephaïs."

Despite their efforts, Finn, and the cultist were unable to secure a willing captain. After searching multiple sea taverns, they sought refuge for the night at a nearby inn of the cultist's choosing. Which, to Finn's bemusement, was tended by a cat.

Fortunately, the cultist had come prepared for such a journey. Armed with rapport and a story of his latest conquest over the Zoogs, the cultist secured a room by trading a meager amount of spice with the cat. Soon thereafter, he and Finn were seated at a table by torchlight, at the inn's Somnium Lounge, deliberating how best to proceed.

Eyes and ears were upon them at once, and hushed whispers spread amongst the patrons who couldn't help but eavesdrop on the madmen seeking passage to Celephaïs.

The fallen city appeared to have been abandoned by seafarers and feared by all, with many a crew remaining docked for extended periods in Thran. None even dared to continue their once convenient routes with the nearest trading city of Hlanith, for fear it would fall next.

"Someone will take us," the cultist said. His hand disappeared beneath the table, and when it emerged, it held a Night-gaunt hook which had been transformed into a menacing blade. Placing the blade on the table in front of Finn, he added, "this inn was not chosen at random. We came here for this ancient blade, hidden by my brethren."

Finn examined the blade, a skeptical frown on his face. "I'm no good with weapons, and I'm not comfortable carrying one."

"This blade," the cultist whispered, sliding it closer to Finn, "is far from ordinary. The Great One demands that you wield it."

"Why?" Finn asked, his voice trembling.

"It will protect you on our journey to Celephaïs."

"That's your job."

"You've nearly lost your life already," the cultist said. "I can only do so much."

"Then you wield it."

59

The cultist grinned, running his finger across the bevel of the blade. "Once activated, your blade can vanquish even the mightiest Dreamlandians. Furthermore, any non-resident dreamer who falls victim to its lethal edge will be exiled from the Dreamlands forever."

"I won't hurt anyone."

"They'll hurt you," the cultist snapped. "Do you remember what happens if you die?"

Finn nodded. If the cultist's words were true, death in the Dreamlands would condemn him to an eternity of serving the daemon-sultan Azathoth, suffering unimaginable torment. "You said the blade is only effective once activated."

Before the cultist could answer, a bone-chilling draft swept through the room. The cultist stood and grabbed the blade, sheathing it at his side as a stranger approached their table.

The torchlight flickered at the stranger's presence, and the ancient tapestry which hung from the wall beside them fluttered as though touched by an unseen breeze.

"Greetings, travelers," the stranger intoned, extending a hand from within his tattered robe of midnight blue. "You seek the fallen city of Celephaïs, in Ooth-Nargai beyond the Tanarian Hills, where reigned the great King Kuranes."

The cultist and Finn exchanged glances, neither daring to reach out and take the withered hand which hung in the air before them.

"Where *reigns* the great King Kuranes," the cultist said as he sat back down.

Their server approached, balancing a tray filled with steaming food, stealing Finn's attention. The stranger turned to the server and flicked his wrist with such command that the man turned tail and hurried away.

Finn's eyes followed the server with longing as he disappeared through the batwing doors to the kitchen, leaving behind nothing but a trail of tantalizing aromas.

The cultist shot a glance at Finn, his eyes calling out. *We mustn't trust this man.*

"Why not?" Finn asked.

The cultist was taken aback by Finn's response, glaring with intense hostility. Finn's head snapped to the side, his eyes widening as he registered the fact that the cultist's lips had not moved, nor uttered a single word.

Finn had tapped into the cultists' inner thoughts, as if they were being whispered into his ear. When Finn turned back to the stranger, he was met with a raised eyebrow and a wide grin, the stranger's hand still outstretched in a welcoming gesture.

"Come, my friends," the stranger urged, "my brigantine awaits." Then, with deliberate intent, he planted thoughts for Finn to internalize. *The tides of fate await no mortal hesitation. You are indeed required in Celephaïs.*

Finn closed his eyes, feeling a shiver run down his spine and sending a chill through his body. *I can hear their intentions*, he realized. *Nyar's words were true.* As he listened, the innermost thoughts of both the cultist and stranger unfolded before him.

In that moment, he trusted in the cultist's intention to safeguard him. While in the stranger's thoughts, he heard nothing but a genuine intention to deliver them both to Celephaïs.

Finn took the stranger's hand and gave it a dignified shake. "We set sail in the morning."

With a glance of malice, the cultist tossed a bag of spice upon the wooden table, a good faith payment as must be customary of such ventures.

When the stranger reached for the bag, however, the cultist retrieved the Night-gaunt blade, stabbing it into the pouch and spilling the precious spice into the deep wood grains of the table.

Finn didn't require any special insight to determine the cultist's intentions. Should the stranger betray them, or hinder their journey to the shores of Celephaïs, the cultist would put an end to his being.

THE VOYAGE

THE BRIGANTINE GLIDED over the river, guided by the stranger and his skeleton crew. As promised, they met Finn and the cultist first thing in the morning and wasted no time setting sail. By late day, their ship had sailed past the fragrant jungles of Kled, immersing Finn in the intoxicating scents of exotic flora, and it continued at a steady pace throughout the night, passing unseen mysteries until the next morning, when Finn rose to see the river widen.

Soon thereafter, cottages were spotted along the banks, followed by walls of rugged granite and fantastic houses with beamed and plastered gables.

The cultist recognized the area as Hlanith, a once bustling trading city at the mouth of the river, where it met the vast expanse of the Cerenerian sea. Presuming Hlanith, like Thran, was closed to most business. They did not stop for trade or food, feasting instead on the stranger's supply of salted meats and stale bread.

The river led next into the Cerenerian sea, and the brigantine sliced through its first shimmering swell with precision, maneuvered by the strangers' small but capable crew. Apart from the cultist and Finn, the crew comprised only a first mate, helmsman, lookout, and a sailor who was tirelessly tending to the ropes and riggings.

Over two nights and two days, the ship pressed on, cutting through the waves of the Cerenerian sea, while Finn yearned for a glimpse of land. Alas, as the second day wore on, his hopes were answered by the outline of a distant mountain.

"Mount Aran welcomes us," the cultist said. "As do the pristine marble walls, gleaming bronze statues, and rolling green hills of Celephaïs."

"But it's fallen," Finn said.

"The citizens of Thran are misguided; the picturesque city remains untarnished."

"I assure you; it is not as you remember," the stranger said.

The cultist fixed his gaze on Finn. "King Kuranes is an extraordinary dreamer. He would not allow the glorious city of his creation to fall."

"Despite all the beauty and splendor King Kuranes imagined," the stranger said, "He longs for the English countryside of his youth with such fervor that he would forsake it all."

"Not destroy it," the cultist replied.

The stranger grinned, his yellow and black teeth on full display. "What if such a powerful dreamer were to conjure nightmares?"

"Are you implying the king is behind this?"

"Not at all."

"Then hold your tongue, stranger."

Finn changed the subject. "What is our true mission in Celephaïs?"

"We are here to seek the king," the cultist said. "My elders have spoken to him before."

Finn kept it to himself, but the sight of Mount Aran's peak brought forth an unsettling sense of familiarity. He believed it was the same peak shown to him by Nyarlathotep, above which the nightmares were forming. "And the blade you've asked me to carry?"

"You will need it yet; we will activate it once we learn how."

Underneath the cultist's words, Finn sensed a flicker of doubt. When he focused on the cultist's mind using his newfound ability, he found the man's thoughts were filled with nothing but questions and overwhelming doubts.

Have the lands fallen, the cultist wondered, *and what are we to do upon reaching the shore?*

The cultist's heart grew uneasy each time he looked at the approaching land. It was then that Finn realized the cultist's vagueness was not a deliberate ploy; he knew little of their mission, or the Great One he worshipped so. He only knew that he had been tasked with leading Finn into the eye of this storm, a task accepted with blind faith.

From the crow's nest, the lookout's voice echoed, "vessel sighted, two points off starboard bow!"

The first mate, with a wicked grin, barked orders for his crew to prepare for battle. The helmsman adjusted course while the sailor raised a flag, its black fabric billowing in the rising winds, displaying the fearsome Jolly Roger insignia.

"This is a pirate ship?" Finn asked.

The stranger's toothy grin grew wider. "Who else would transport outsiders to the depths of hell?"

It took time to reach the other vessel, time which filled Finn's heart with fear. He and the cultist were powerless to fight the pirate crew, nor could they sail a ship if they were to orchestrate a successful uprising.

With the winds intensifying and the swells growing choppy, their ship surged forward towards its target, surrounded by the encroaching darkness.

Soon, the gap between the ships was bridged. The opposing vessel did not evade, however. Even as the skeleton crew barked threats of violence at them, the vessel kept position.

Finn scanned the vessel's deck, spotting no signs of movement.

"They've gone below deck," the lookout announced.

"Cowards," the first mate snorted as he launched his grappling hook with precision, lodging it into the rail of the drifting vessel as he called to his crew. "Secure the line."

With a united effort, the pirates gathered around the line, their hands joining to create a powerful force as they heaved with all their strength. Amidst the grunts and strains of their efforts, the vessel drifted closer, until they were mere inches apart.

The ships collided, and a violent pitch knocked Finn off his feet. His head struck the deck. The cultist clung to the brigantine's rails, his hands trembling, while the stranger, frail as he was, maintained his posture, his wicked grin never faltering.

Finn climbed to his feet and braced himself against the rail. Though his eyes were clouded from the trauma, he could see that the pirate crew fared much better. They ran crouched to maintain balance and swarmed the opposing deck.

As the pirates searched the vessel, Finn spotted jagged, mucus laden spines peeking out from the companionway hatch, testing the air as though they smelt the invading pirates.

"Get off the ship," Finn screamed.

The hatch swung open, revealing a horrendous creature. Its elongated torso coiled like that of a serpent, exposing rows of sharp, serrated fins that writhed with a sickening grace as it shot into the sky.

The creature was both quick and silent. For the pirates remained oblivious to its presence as it approached them from behind. Finn called out again, but his voice couldn't carry over the crash of the swells against the ships' hulls.

Only the serpent heard his screams. It turned its bulbous, milky eyes towards Finn, which peeked out from beneath a layer of crusty scales. The eyes were hypnotic, holding Finn in place, and urging him to witness the terrifying sight.

The serpent positioned itself behind the first mate, its

spine-laden maw dripping with anticipation. Then it lunged forth, skewering the pirate with a vicious strike and hoisting his lifeless body into the air.

Weapons drawn; the pirates congregated beneath globs of salivate which slopped onto the deck as their first mate was devoured.

Finn ducked, retrieved the Night-gaunt blade sheathed at his side, and tried to ignore the piercing screams. *If only I knew how to activate this damn thing.*

The screaming stopped, prompting Finn to peer over the rail. What greeted him was a nightmare. A macabre display of anatomical distortion. The bodies of each pirate were contorted. What remained of their faces twisted in agony. Limbs detached, stretched, or strung together by sinew and tendon. Blood dripped from every surface of the brigantine, pooling in viscous puddles upon the deck, and the creature had vanished.

Chanting rose from the cultist's position. He was clutching his rectangular charm, knuckles white, as if he were preparing for an imminent explosion similar to the one that had decimated the Zoogs.

"If you're planning something," Finn cried. "Do it now!"

The silence in the air became absolute as they waited for the serpent's inevitable re-emergence. Finn heard his own heartbeat in his chest and felt each thump pounding in his head. His eyes darted in every direction.

It wasn't until he heard the drip of water falling from the creature that Finn realized where it was, and by then, it was too late. Rising from the sea, the creature's monstrous, serpent-like body loomed over him, a chilling re-enactment of its earlier strike upon the first mate.

This is it. Finn squeezed his eyes shut and held his breath.

"I will return for you," the cultist shouted, his hurried footsteps pounding on the deck.

Finn stood frozen, transfixed by the creature's gaping maw and the sharp, prickly spines within.

With a swift movement, the cultist pushed Finn aside and hurled himself into the serpent's mouth. The startled creature let out a symphony of painful cries as the cultist forced himself through its gullet.

The cultist soon vanished, and in an instant, his amulet glowed from within the serpent, igniting a path through its writhing torso. The serpent hissed, its spines protruding from its mouth as it lunged towards Finn.

A second surge of energy erupted. The writhing serpent burst open, showering the brigantine in a tidal wave of foul-smelling chum, as its motionless, scaly head crashed down on Finn, trapping him in place.

Even in death, the serpent's milky eyes bore into Finn's soul, just as repulsive and terrifying as they had been in life.

Such a monster could only be described as a nightmare, which meant they were nearing the rift. Strange and unsettling creatures would continue to slither from the sky above Mount Aran until the whole of the land was consumed.

"The shore awaits, traveler." The stranger approached. He reached down and retrieved the Night-gaunt blade from the deck beside Finn, his eyes fixated on its shimmering surface.

"Please," Finn gasped, his voice strained, "I can't breathe. This thing is crushing me."

"Then I suggest you start cutting," the stranger said, handing Finn the blade. With a snap of his fingers, the stranger vanished in a wisp of shadow, leaving Finn to struggle beneath the creature's weight.

Rest Now, Frances

NYARLATHOTEP MATERIALIZED BESIDE Frances, his spectral wisps slithering around the cathedral's chancel, which had grown nauseating with the stench of death since his departure. The congealed blood, the foul reek of expelled bowels, and the lingering odor of extinguished torches assaulted the senses, but Frances remained unfazed, her mind resolute.

Nyarlathotep had skirted her question regarding his need for her, but in a gesture of good faith, communed to the Dreamlands to monitor Finn's progress. The only thing Frances cared about now was the news that the shadow entity had brought back in the hour since his departure. A span of time, which in the Dreamlands could equate to any stretch.

But before she could utter a word of question, Nyarlathotep pinched his fingers shut, sealing her mouth from afar. In the same motion, he directed his hand towards the podium before her, where she noticed the young cultist rousing.

"Take his life," Nyarlathotep commanded.

Frances narrowed her eyes and studied Nyarlathotep. Just an hour prior, she had been denied ending this man's life. "What's different now?"

"Do not question me, Frances." Nyarlathotep pointed at the blood-stained flail, which lay next to the severed head of a slain cultist. "Kill him."

The cultist was in a daze, unaware of his surroundings or the conversation regarding his fate.

Frances lifted the flail from the ground, but she couldn't shake the overwhelming sense of guilt. "This cultist was deemed of value, someone who would protect Finn."

"His purpose has been fulfilled."

"You had no problem disposing of the other cultists. Why don't you kill him?"

"This one's mind is powerful; he needs to be silenced in a way that I cannot command. My earthly interventions are less than physical."

As Frances wiped the crusted blood from the flail's spikes, she couldn't help but wonder why she resisted. Her first instinct had been to eliminate the cultist and revel in the aftermath. But now that Nyarlathotep was compelling her, she was reluctant.

"Before anything," Frances said, "I want to question him."

"You mustn't."

"Then I'll question you." Frances turned her flail towards Nyarlathotep. "When Finn has served his purpose, would you eliminate him?"

"Finn's continued existence is all that matters."

Doubt lingered in Frances' mind, but between the Cthulhu Cult and Nyarlathotep, she trusted the latter more. She clenched her teeth and mustered her courage, swinging the flail above her head with increasing force and velocity as the cultist sat upright on the podium.

The cultist's eyes snapped open, only to be greeted by the sight of a spiked ball barreling towards him. As Frances' flail struck his skull, a sharp crack echoed through the air, like the sound of a bowling ball hitting a lone pin.

His skull shattered, fragments piercing the delicate brain tissue it once shielded. Blood spurted from the wound, drenching the young man's face as his eyes, bloodshot and vacant, rolled back in his head. His lifeless body fell back onto the podium, taking the flail with it.

"I've done as you've asked," Frances said. "Now tell me why."

Nyarlathotep left the altar, seeking refuge from the overpowering stench of death that filled the chancel, and took a seat in the rear pews. "The cultist possessed an artifact vital to Finn's quest. Now that Finn has received the artifact, he is free to continue his journey alone."

Frances' footsteps echoed through the cathedral as she followed. "Without protection?"

Nyarlathotep nodded, his grin spreading from ear to ear—a sinister expression reminiscent of a deranged lunatic. "Finn's abilities are awakening. Before he can come into his own and protect others, he must first learn to become his own guardian."

Frances knew she would not receive any simple answers from Nyarlathotep, but her questions continued to multiply. What was Finn up against in the Dreamlands, and what artifact did the Cthulhu Cult possess which would be vital to his success?

"Take me to the Dreamlands," Frances said. "My son is out there, confused and alone."

Nyar crossed his legs and sank into the pew. "Finn will not be alone for long. Rest now, Frances," he said, closing his eyes. "Everything will unfold accordingly. You must save your strength for what awaits on the horizon, for that is where your greatest challenges lie."

CELEPHAÏS

WET SAND MOLDED to Finn's feet as he pushed off the sea floor, navigating through the rough, churning waves by the light of the stars above. After an arduous swim from the disabled brigantine, his exhausted body trembled with a cold which could not be dispelled.

He kept pushing. The water level fell below his knees, and the shore lay just ahead. He sprinted as the waters receded, collapsing onto the sand, allowing the deep ache in his muscles to receive a well-earned reprieve.

There was little time to rest, however. Celephaïs, a place which once held such beauty as to inspire the cultist's countless tales and legends, had indeed fallen. There would be no escape from the constant terror that loomed over him.

In the city's backdrop, Finn spotted silhouettes of both movement and inanimate destruction, the likes of which could not have been wrought by mere mortals. The sort of writhing, slithering monsters he feared were spilling out from the sky above.

A path of slain bodies lined the beach, leading up to toppled minarets and crumbled stone that stood as a grim reminder of the challenges ahead. Some of the fallen were human-like, others alien and several monstrous in proportion.

Statues of gold and bronze reflected the starlight and bore the scars of war. Oxidation had darkened their surfaces, while heat reduced their once symmetrical depictions to twisted shapes that seemed to cry out into the night. The city was a significant departure from the idealized and faultless land the cultist had described.

Worse yet were the noises. Sounds that squelched and carried throughout the salty breeze. Finn found himself surrounded by eerie noises he could not identify—a flutter of membranous wings, a hiss whizzing past his ears, a shriek which faded into oblivion.

Madness surrounded him. He turned, sensing a sound low and guttural. But darkness greeted his vision. Retrieving the blade from its sheath, Finn spun in all directions, attempting to locate the sound which bellowed from the depths before choosing to flee.

Echoes chased him through the night, sending shivers down his spine as he approached the fallen structures of stone. He searched for a haven amongst the ruin, somewhere to hide from whatever was closing in on his position. But the sound grew closer, discordant, like the dissonant notes of a devil's symphony.

Ahead, amidst a pile of large stone, was a fallen minaret. Finn sheathed his blade and squeezed through a narrow crack in the stone. Once through, there was a clearing beneath the minaret's toppled dome where he could take cover.

He hunkered down, and that's when he felt it. Vibrations coursing through the sand. As the dirt piled up around him, Finn realized that the disturbance was coming from below.

A massive pincer erupted through the surface and seized Finn's leg. With a tight squeeze, the chela severed his flesh, causing intense agony as his muscles and tendons retreated. The wound gushed blood, splattering the giant claw with a fresh crimson hue.

Hand over hand, Finn pulled himself across the beach, through the labyrinth of toppled stone as his vision blackened. The oversized crustacean breached in its

72

entirety, launching the minaret's dome into the air as it displaced tons of sand.

Finn rolled, dodging falling stones as they crashed down around him. With each motion, his severed thigh leaked more blood. In this state, he knew he wouldn't survive for long; he needed to find a hiding place, but it seemed luck had abandoned him.

He rolled onto his back, awaiting the crustacean's deadly attack. When in the same instant, a piercing screech echoed through the sky above. It was the unmistakable battle cry of the Night-gaunt which had plagued his journey from the get-go.

The winged creature soared overhead with a speed and aptitude the crustacean could not match, targeting weak spots like a precision scalpel. In a series of swift, repeated motions, the Night-gaunt pierced the cartilage between the crustacean's joints, exposing the tender white flesh beneath.

The crustacean flailed, emitting a frantic clicking sound. Its right pincer hung by a thread of tissue.

Finn's vision flickered like a strobe light, fragmenting the scene before him. Flashes of the Night-gaunt streaked across the sky as its hooks tore into the crustacean's eyes, causing sprays of goop to cascade over the beach.

The Night-gaunt, seizing its opponent's blindness, landed beside Finn, drawing nearer with quick jerking movements. Draped from the Night-gaunt's neck was his amulet, confirmation that this was the same creature that had attacked him prior.

With a trembling hand, Finn reached out in vain, but the amulet eluded his grasp. The Night-gaunt lingered over him, and as his vision faded, he felt the sharp sting of its hooks as they pierced the sand and wrapped around his back. His body was lifted into the air as he once again succumbed to unconsciousness.

THE SAVIOR

WATER DRIPPED OVER Finn's face, rousing him from his unconscious state. Massive rock formations loomed around him, their surfaces slick with mist. Underneath him was a straw-like material comprising a bed. With a sense of disbelief, he looked down and saw that his leg had been reconnected.

He peeled off the unfamiliar pants that he had been dressed in, his eyes drawn at once to the wound—a thick, bulbous line of pink which circled his thigh, marking the spot where his leg had been severed, yet it showed signs of months-long healing.

A nearby voice called out, "Finn, you're awake."

The voice was soon accompanied by its speaker, a middle-aged man, who wore clothes similar to those Finn was dressed in. The clothing was brown and basic, made from thick thread. It was the style of garb one would imagine a medieval peasant wearing.

"Who are you?" Finn asked.

The man knelt, allowing for a better view of his face. "You must know who I am."

Finn blinked, investigating the man's facial features, and sure enough, he recognized them. Not from any previous interaction, but from the photographs his mother displayed throughout their house.

This was the face behind all the stories he had heard as a child. It was the face of the man who inspired him to save the world in the first place.

"You look just like my dad, Donnie . . . "

"Dad is fine."

This is a delusion, Finn thought. He sat upright, *a chaotic misfiring of neurons. Azathoth's eternal torture,* perhaps. "My father died before I was born. He never knew my mom was pregnant. You can't be him."

"Can't I?"

"My father wouldn't know my name, or anything about me."

Donnie smiled, his eyes alive with curiosity. "Yet I do. Tell me, son, what does death mean?"

Finn tried to reconcile the cryptic response with his experiences since arriving in the Dreamlands, which had been anything but ordinary. "I don't know what death means. Reality doesn't even make sense these days."

"Well, these lands are quite real. Filled with powerful dreamers, some of whom remained here in spirit, even after expiring in the waking world."

"Like King Kuranes?"

"There are passages between our worlds, windows through which information can be gleaned. Let's just say you've never been alone, son." Donnie wrapped his arms around Finn and held him tight. "I've kept my eye on you these many years, and I've waited for this moment longer than you can imagine."

Finn shuddered, wondering if this man was one of Nyarlathotep's illusions. But when they were locked in an embrace, an undeniable sensation of belonging washed over him. He couldn't explain why, but he knew beyond any doubt that this man was his father.

"You don't know how long I've waited for this." Finn tightened his hold on Donnie. "My entire life, I've dreamed of this moment." After an extended embrace, Finn released his arms and looked down at the scar around his thigh. "How did you . . . "

"There are many healing tools in these lands, if you

know how to exploit them. You've been asleep for some time thanks to the potent leaves of the moonflower."

Finn shot to his feet, realizing that time's passage all but ensured an onslaught of nightmares had breached the rift. "It's not safe here," he said, as his leg gave out and sent him to the ground.

From of the corner of Finn's eye, he saw the Night-gaunt snap into view. It lowered its head and raced towards him. But rather than attack, the Night-gaunt slid a horn under Finn's arm, helping him to stand.

"That thing is yours?" Finn asked.

Donnie reached out his hand and pet the creature's wet, rubbery skin. "Whom do you think brought you here?"

The Night-gaunt flapped its membranous wings in response, kicking its leg.

"It stole my amulet," Finn said.

Donnie removed Finn's amulet from around the Night-gaunt's neck. "Sometimes Night-gaunt's have a mind of their own," he said. "Which is fortunate, otherwise you may never have found me here."

"Where is here?"

"Mount Aran, and there is much work to be done." Donnie placed the amulet around Finn's neck. "Look," he said, his eyes burning with excitement. "It glows."

Finn hesitated, remembering this was a world of delusion. "The amulet is part of *my* quest." He patted the pockets of his new pants, finding them all to be empty. "What have you done with my blade?"

Donnie reached behind his back, "do not worry," he said, detaching a sheath from his pants. "I have the blade. I didn't want you to hurt yourself."

Finn reached for the blade, but his father pulled it away.

"None of this is what you expected," Donnie said, his voice filled with a mixture of sorrow and remorse, as he unsheathed the Night-gaunt blade. "We've been cast into an extraordinary and time sensitive situation."

"We have."

Turning the blade over in his hands, Donnie regarded the intricate symbols carved into its surface. "Once we've restored order," he continued, "I promise to give you the time and undivided attention you deserve. For now, trust I have been unable to reach you."

The Night-gaunt squawked, its head jerking as it moved closer to Finn. Before Finn could react, the Night-gaunt's winged limbs wrapped around him, locking him in place.

Donnie grabbed Finn's wrist, his grip tightening as he pressed the blade into the palm of Finn's hand, causing a sharp, searing pain, and a deluge of blood. Then he wiped the blade in the blood, ensuring every inch of its shining surface was coated.

"You are more powerful than you know," Donnie said, releasing his grip.

The blade's surface burst into flame, its intricate symbols radiating a dazzling golden glow that cut through the crimson stain of blood. Eventually, the fires subsided, leaving behind only a faint glow that persisted within the blades' eldritch insignia.

"This blade holds great power," Donnie said, calling on his Night-gaunt companion to release Finn. "Power that can only be awakened by the most exceptional beings."

Finn felt a surge of betrayal. "You've got what you wanted, then."

"I've had access to your blood. I wanted you to witness the activation." Donnie sheathed the blade and handed it to Finn. "This belongs to you. Only a resident Dreamlandian may wield it, or one who has been assimilated."

"What are you, then?"

"I am an entity whose physical form exists outside the boundaries of this realm."

"But your spirit remained here, like King Kuranes'."

Donnie shook his head. "I never said that. You assumed, and I did not correct you."

Finn attached the blade to his pants, eyeing his father. "If you're communing here, then your body lives in the waking world . . ."

"It does."

"But mom . . . " Finn tried to quell the unpleasant feelings brewing inside of him. "She's been suffering for twenty years. She thinks you're dead. My whole life *I* thought you were dead. How dare you lie to us!"

ℐT IS ℐIME

NYARLATHOTEP OPENED HIS EYES, gazing out over the cathedral pews. It was the moment Frances had been waiting for. She was trapped, forced to endure the overwhelming stench of death in the cold, foreboding cathedral as he slept.

Nyarlathotep, she presumed, spent his shuteye communing to the Dreamlands, not in presence, but in spirit, to observe Finn's quest from afar.

"It's time I returned to the Dreamlands," Nyarlathotep said. "You've served your son well, though I cannot say the same for his father."

Frances stiffened, feeling a mixture of shock and disbelief at the mention of her late husband. "Donnie died on R'lyeh," she said, her voice trembling.

"You needn't play dumb, Frances."

"What do you mean?"

"Rest now. I will return for you," Nyarlathotep insisted.

"You're taking me with you to the Dreamlands. My son needs me."

"Then why did you not prepare him?" Nyarlathotep stood, straightened his attire, and raised his head with an indignant glare. "You may not have known *what* was coming, but you knew from *who* Finn came."

"Donnie?"

Nyarlathotep stared blankly.

"Donnie was a saint," she cried. "He was a marine

biologist. A husband. A father who never got to meet his son. I told Finn everything about him."

Nyarlathotep raised his hands, his fingers trembling as he summoned blinding light into them. "You do not remember," he said, wrapping his lanky fingers around her skull. "You must have repressed the trauma." He pushed his fingertips deep into her temples. "Allow me to refresh your memory, Frances."

THE RIFT

FINN, WITH RELUCTANCE, led his father and the Night-gaunt up Mount Aran's treacherous ascent, navigating slick rock and scaling loose boulders. The answers he sought from his father were on hold; less important than locating the rift. So he bit his tongue and trudged onward, following the amulet's direction.

The air grew thin, insubstantial. Breathing was no longer automatic; it required deliberate effort. Finn forced the frigid air through his nose, down into his lungs. With each step, his heartbeat became louder, and his head felt more detached.

Mount Aran was a vast landscape. They reached the summit and still had an endless plateau to conquer. Mist and clouds hung in the air, making it difficult to see, but in between their billows, the rift made itself visible at last.

Finn's amulet shone brighter than ever before. It physically tugged at him, urging him to traverse the plateau. "I know we're short on time," Finn said, facing his father. "But if we're going to die, I need to know why you left us . . . What were you doing here?"

"I was doing what needed to be done."

Finn clenched his fists. "Which didn't involve your family."

"Why did you come here?" Donnie asked.

"I didn't come here," Finn said, recalling his talk with Nyarlathotep. "I was led here."

"Because you're my son." Pride shone through

Donnie's eyes. "Our minds are our greatest assets. Even our physical weapons," he said, pointing to the Night-gaunt blade at Finn's side, "are useless without our thoughts."

Finn strained to read his father's intentions the way he had with the cultist and the stranger, but there was an impenetrable barrier. "Why would *our* thoughts hold such power?"

"Becau—"

The Night-gaunt let out an ear-splitting screech, cutting Donnie's response short. It bolted across the landscape, rocks flying from beneath its hooked feet.

Donnie took off after his pet, "hurry, he's on the trail."

Finn watched his father and the Night-gaunt disappear into the mist. Though he didn't need his eyes to find them, only his amulet. Sure enough, it led him to the same patch of electrified air that the Night-gaunt had taken his father to.

"The amulet," Donnie said. "It will direct you to the proper location."

Static lifted Finn's hair as he neared the disturbance. The amulet hummed, reverberating through his chest. Ahead, the air crackled with lightning and smelled of fire. It was not, however, the rift which he was drawn to. This was something else altogether.

The disturbance reminded him of the fabric he had encountered around Thran. This must be what Nyar was leading him to, and the reason both his father and the Night-gaunt sought the aid of his amulet.

Finn's heart pounded. In this moment, every aspect of his quest came together, filling the air with a sense of anticipation and purpose. He reached for the disturbance, inserted his hands into the flickering fabric and pulled, but Donnie dragged him back.

"Beyond this illusion is the source of the rift," Donnie said. "The birthplace of nightmares. There is no time for hesitation. The weapon you wield is the only object in this, or any universe, which can help. You must be strong. Strong in your resolve and unyielding in your approach. You must silence this monster before everything is lost."

Donnie stepped away, allowing Finn to pull back the illusory cloak.

A broken man was knelt within. His shoulders hunched, his body shaking with uncontrollable madness. Burdened by the weight of the world, his eyes were rolled back, revealing only their whites, giving him an eerie and unsettling appearance, while a golden crown rested upon his head.

Finn clutched the Night-gaunt blade in his hand, shifting his gaze to Donnie. "You want me to kill King Kuranes?"

REPRESSED MEMORIES

FRANCES FOUND HERSELF at Nyarlathotep's mercy, unable to escape his sinister grasp. His fingers were laid upon her head, radiating an intense, pulsating energy that awakened the dormant pathways in her mind.

She did not know if those mental connections had been severed due to trauma or if they were removed intentionally. Regardless, after two decades, she was about to recount in detail the troubling moments which ensued after Cthulhu captured her on R'lyeh.

Cthulhu's tentacles seized Frances and Donnie. Armed with a fire axe, she locked eyes with her husband, knowing no matter what came of their lives, her heart always belonged to him.

Donnie smiled back, conveying a declaration of love. He prepared his spear gun and, with the pull of the trigger, pierced Cthulhu's right eye.

Cthulhu shrieked in agony. His grip on her and Donnie tightened, suffocating them. Knowing the end was soon, Frances used the last of her strength to mouth the words 'I love you.'

That much she knew, but she never expected the memory which came next.

Cthulhu's tentacles tightened around Donnie, constricting until his face turned blue. The sickening crunch of bone filled Frances' ears. Blood poured from Donnie's mouth, the same mouth which had just smiled at her.

Through a kaleidoscope of tears, she watched Cthulhu's massive tentacles fling Donnie's lifeless body into the sea, where he took his place amongst the burning wreckage and floating corpses.

The fire axe fell from Frances' hands, splashing into the waters below as Cthulhu carried her back to his pit in R'lyeh. The creature was delicate thereafter, as she had given up the struggle, subdued by the fact that she was powerless to stop him.

That's when it happened. Cthulhu uncoiled his hectocotylus—an arm used by cephalopods to transfer sperm. A term she only knew from Donnie's career as a marine biologist. It was something she never imagined encountering in this capacity.

Frances broke free from Nyarlathotep's grasp. "Stop, I don't want to see any more."

Tears welled in her eyes. Finn was not the result of her and Donnie's love. Nor was he the legacy of her late husband. He was an otherworldly being, possessing god-like powers and unlimited potential. Potential, which they had both been blind to.

"Cthulhu has taken Donnie's form to set Finn's mind at ease," Nyarlathotep snapped his fingers, initiating his disappearance. "He has not left R'lyeh, because he has been building an army to obliterate existence as we know it."

"But Finn knows Donnie is dead."

"Despite his abilities, Finn has been unable to discern the lie, because Cthulhu is his true father."

Frances took hold of Nyarlathotep, wrapping her arms around him as the shadow entity disassembled. "You're not leaving without me."

"Your body will be defenseless," he warned. "Your mind will be assimilated and vulnerable."

Frances disregarded Nyarlathotep's warning, her senses overwhelmed by the shadows ripping the consciousness from her body, fragment by fragment, pulling her mind inexorably into the Dreamlands.

Cthulhu killed her husband, impregnated her, and now the creature threatened to destroy her son. She didn't know what she would do when she reached Cthulhu, but she needed to ensure his death.

KILL THE KING

INN HAD NEVER killed a man; nor dreamt of such a thing. King Kuranes was a ragged and helpless shell, whose mind had been consumed by something unknown. Yet the king's nightmares, Donnie explained, unleashed this dreadful fate upon the Dreamlands.

Only several of the king's monsters had escaped the rift thus far, the nimblest forms slipping through tiny gaps in the sky's fabric, and their destruction was immeasurable. Soon the rift would burst, releasing a surge of nightmares that would annihilate both the Dreamlands and the waking world.

With the Night-gaunt blade in his hand, Finn pondered whether to use its power to slay the king or conjure another solution. The weight of such a decision was more than he wished to carry, but as the wielder of the blade, the choice was his to make.

Finn stared at King Kuranes, then at his father, who nodded in approval. He raised the blade high, preparing to put an end to the madness, but the Night-gaunt panicked. It thrashed its wings and knocked the blade from his hand.

"Infernal beast," Donnie thundered at the Night-gaunt. His words dripping with contempt as he directed his ire onto Finn. "Pick up the blade, damnit. End this."

Before Finn could retrieve the blade, a wisp of shadow appeared before him and materialized into two distinct beings: a tall, peculiar-looking man, who he could only

87

presume was Nyarlathotep's preferred guise, and his mother.

Finn watched his mother march up to Donnie and land a powerful blow.

"This was your plan all along," she shouted. "To create a hybrid being to serve your will." She looked back at Finn with pride in her eyes. "My son knows right from wrong."

Nyarlathotep surrounded Finn in shadow, creating a barrier between him and King Kuranes.

"What the hell is going on?" Finn demanded.

"Cthulhu seized control of the king's mind," Nyarlathotep explained. "Compelling him to dream of unspeakable horrors, knowing they would manifest into being." He kneeled beside the trembling king. "Kuranes hid himself beneath the rift, where he could fight a mental battle, holding the nightmares at bay, to the determinant of his sanity."

Finn picked the Night-gaunt blade off the ground. "We must stop the dreaming."

"The king's mind is the only thread holding the rift together," Nyarlathotep insisted. "Sever it and chaos will consume everything in its path."

Finn looked at his mother. "Dad says we need to stop the king."

She looked back at Finn, tears running down her face. "That's not the dad you know, and my name isn't Emma-Lynn, son. No more lies. My name is Frances Smith. I released Cthulhu," she said, looking towards Donnie. "This is my fault."

"You're not my dad?" Finn asked, facing Donnie.

Donnie's skin stretched and contorted, shattering the avatar's illusion. The transformation was horrifying to witness. Flesh tore apart, giving way to a slimy, gelatinous mass of tentacles nestled beneath.

"I am your father," he said, in a voice deep and sinister, "but I am not Donnie Smith."

Finn felt ill as the unspoken truth dawned on him.

Frances Smith's provocative journal entries. The tentacles writhing beneath his father's disguise . . .

Human societies and institutions were never meant for him. He was an alien, living amongst a culture to which he did not belong. Cthulhu's history, which he felt inclined to study, was his birthright. His flesh but a shell, like Cthulhu's avatar, concealing the creature within.

Cthulhu's telepathic voice echoed in his mind. *You are a god. We were made to rule together, but you must kill the king.*

The Night-gaunt blade glowed, begging to rend flesh. Its power was hypnotic, but Finn fought its allure. He needed to decide whether killing the king would stop the nightmares or unleash them en mass.

"All three of you manipulated me," Finn said. "You've lied about who you are, what you want, and who I am." The more enraged he got, the more he felt his body morph, expressing the helplessness he had never been able to conceptualize. "You all want me to serve your will. How could I trust any of you?"

Frances spoke, her eyes filled with sorrow. "Don't trust us, Finn. Trust yourself."

"I don't know how."

Finn fell to his knees. The overwhelming fear and uncertainty awakening something deep inside, unleashing an innate ability to manifest the dormant creature within. The blade fell. His fingers twisted into awkward tentacles. Slime dripped from his every pore as the fleshy wrapping of his Dreamland presence gave way.

Frances looked at Nyarlathotep. "What's happening to him?"

"He is awakening."

Finn's figure grew massive, contorting into a horrifying visage of Cthulhu, which rose above the clouds. His lips contorted, hardening into a grotesque beak with sharp, serrated teeth.

Cthulhu's intention resonated in his mind. *The blade. We cannot let the blade fall to Nyarlathotep.*

Finn spotted Nyarlathotep reaching for the blade. With a quick thrust, he ensnared the shadow entity in one of his tentacles. As he lifted Nyarlathotep off the ground, a surge of power coursed through his body, an incredible sensation he had never felt before.

"I am no longer bound by the will of others."

"It's not too late," Nyarlathotep begged, his voice filled with desperation as he struggled to free himself from Finn's tentacles. "Cthulhu is a visitor here; his mind is in an ongoing battle with the king's. You can defeat him."

Frances seized on the chaos, retrieving the blade as she bolted across the mountainous terrain. The Night-gaunt took flight and hovered close behind her. Enraged, Cthulhu lashed out with a massive tentacle. It struck Frances and sent her tumbling over the rocks. Her body went limp, and the blade fell from her grasp.

Finn dropped Nyarlathotep and wrestled Cthulhu to the ground, sending quakes through the mountain. Cthulhu rose, striking back at Finn. Each wrestled for the upper hand, tentacles entwined—a writhing mass of muscle and sinew.

Cthulhu's thoughts reached inside Finn as they fought, enlivening his fears and doubts. *You are nothing without me. You will never seal the rift; you'll die just like your parents.*

Finn's grasp weakened, allowing Cthulhu to stagger him with a forceful blow forged in the void of the stars. He fell onto his back, a broken mass of tentacles and bulbous flesh. The impact paralyzing his appendages.

Cthulhu manipulated one of Finn's most slender tentacles, forcing Finn to retrieve the Night-gaunt blade from alongside his mother's body. With a determined grip, Cthulhu pressed Finn to drag the blade towards King Kuranes.

Finn watched, helpless, as the blade ascended into the air. Its power would be enough to kill the king and erase his spirit from the Dreamlands, and if Nyarlathotep were telling the truth, bring about the apocalypse.

Nyarlathotep swooped in at the last moment, riding the Night-gaunt's back. He stole the blade from under King Kuranes' throat and took off into the air. The destiny of their shared existence now hung in the balance, resting in the hands of a deity renowned for his deception.

Cthulhu threw his tentacles into the air, attempting to knock the Night-gaunt out of the sky.

Nyarlathotep jerked the Night-gaunt's head, dodging Cthulhu's attack and initiating a barrel roll through the air. The Night-gaunt leveled out, following a heel from Nyarlathotep. Its wings beat as it maneuvered through the minefield of writhing tentacles, determined to reach Cthulhu's head.

Balanced on the Night-gaunt's back, Nyarlathotep hunched forward, holding the blade in front of him. As the Night-gaunt soared past Cthulhu's bulbous head, the razor-sharp blade found its mark, cutting a line straight through from beak to mantle. A deluge of viscous and blue blood flowed from the wound, toppling Cthulhu.

"He still lives in the waking world," Nyarlathotep bellowed as he soared through the air. "But his mind is exiled from the Dreamlands."

The Night-gaunt touched down, allowing Nyarlathotep to dismount. To Finn's relief, the shadow entity was able to rouse his mother. Then the entity extended his hand to a barely cognizant King Kuranes, helping him rise.

Before long, Nyarlathotep, the king, and Frances were all gathered around Finn's body, which was still immobilized, leaving him to gaze at the rift above.

"Why are the nightmares still here?" Finn asked.

"I have the power to create," the king said, in a weathered voice. "Not to destroy what has been created. I do not know if there is anything which can bring about their end."

"The blade," Finn suggested. "It can destroy them."

Nyarlathotep scoffed. "You believe this one blade can destroy an army of nightmares before they consume every inch of the Dreamlands? Before they penetrate the forbidden passages into the waking world beyond the Tanarian hills?"

The Night-gaunt strode up to Nyarlathotep, nudging his side like a found pet. An affection much stronger than it had shown Cthulhu, which caused Finn to take notice. As he did, he observed something else about the Night-gaunt he hadn't before.

"The Night-gaunt is missing its hook," he said. "I thought the blade was ancient."

Nyarlathotep held the blade fondly as he pet the Night-gaunt's blubbery flesh. "She's an ancient."

Finn began piecing together the vague details of his quest. The Night-gaunt was never Cthulhu's pet. It was Nyarlathotep's servant. A plant designed to confuse Cthulhu, to gain his trust and pretend to aid him until Nyarlathotep's plan could come to fruition.

The amulet, the Night-gaunt, and the ancient blade crafted from its hook. They all tied back to the shadow entity, leaving Finn to wonder how much of his journey had been pre-determined.

"If the blade can't stop them, what can?"

"I told you when we began," Nyarlathotep replied. "You will become one with this world."

Finn closed his eyes, recalling the illusions he had peered through. When he reached his hands into the fabric of reality, they bonded with it. The experience left him feeling as though he would be unable to leave if he lingered any longer. Then he recalled his original vision, gazing upon the Dreamlands from the heavens above, feeling at peace. Like he belonged there.

"My fate is to bind the rift," he said. "To become one with the Dreamlands."

Frances' eyes grew wide. "No! I can't lose you."

"Finn cannot refuse," Nyarlathotep said. "The rift will burst without him. He needs to channel the cosmic energy around him, the way he was born to, the way he has learned to, and in doing so, become the protector of worlds."

Finn summoned strength to his limbs, commanding energy from the Dreamlands as Nyarlathotep instructed, allowing the universe to breathe life into him. Feeling returned to his appendages as his body levitated.

Frances turned to King Kuranes. "There must be another way."

The king looked deep in thought, no doubt racking his brain to devise a more eloquent solution. It was no use, however.

"I love you, Mom." Finn looked down at her as he ascended. "I should have said it more."

"I love you too," Frances cried. "This isn't the end. I'm going to fight."

Her cries grew distant as he ascended further into the sky, his tentacles weaving with the ethereal fabric. They acted as thread, stitching together the breach and becoming one with the vast cosmic tapestry that binds all of existence. Behind him, the nightmares would be forever imprisoned, ensuring the safety of the worlds below.

One day, his mother would understand this was the only way. That the world was better off for it. Perhaps on that day he could narrate a history paper to her from afar, one that would impress Professor Hartfield. For he knew Cthulhu's true intentions. The creature was his father. His intention was to destroy.

THE HORIZON

NYARLATHOTEP TRANSPORTED FRANCES and King Kuranes from the mountaintop, re-materializing together with them in the rose-crystal Palace of the Seventy Delights from which Kuranes had reigned. There was a long road ahead for the shadow entity, as he would be tasked with eliminating the nightmares which had snuck through the rift and still occupied the Dreamlands.

First, however, he needed to decide what would become of the king. "You are the most powerful dreamer," Nyarlathotep said as he locked eyes with King Kuranes. "Even more powerful than Cthulhu. Why did you first yield to the Great One's control?"

"A momentary lapse," the king replied.

"He must have promised you something, something which allowed him into your mind."

King Kuranes looked down in shame, unimpressed with the grand floors of the rose-crystal Palace. Their intricate carvings held no allure for him, nor did the sparkling chandeliers above. They hadn't for some time.

"Cthulhu promised to return me to my home, the English countryside."

"How?" Frances asked. "Your mortal body died."

Nyarlathotep sneered, a malevolent smile spreading across his face as he took a seat at the palace throne. "Mortals . . . There is always a way. There are many bodies to be assumed, many paths to be woven."

King Kuranes maintained a skeptical optimism. "We have not seen eye to eye before. But if you can find it in your heart, to grant this old man his grandest wish."

"Entrust your burdens to me, and I will give you a new life."

King Kuranes' eyes widened with delight. "Thank you. You'll look after the kingdom?"

Nyarlathotep nodded and snapped his fingers. In an instant, a wisp of shadow consumed the king, transporting him to the waking world and leaving only Frances in the Nyarlathotep's care.

"If you're granting wishes, I'd like my son back," Frances said.

"Impossible," Nyarlathotep said as he settled into his throne. "Be happy. Good has triumphed."

Frances eyed Nyarlathotep with a mixture of contempt and admiration. "No, you have triumphed. It took me time to figure out what you were up to, but I see now who you are."

Nyarlathotep smirked. "Oh?"

Frances clenched her fists as she approached his throne. "The only interest you hold in the survival of our worlds is control. You couldn't control the nightmares. Had you let them destroy us, you would have no decent beings left to manipulate."

"Would you have preferred death?"

"You may be able to wield the Night-gaunt blade, but you weren't powerful enough to activate it. You used Finn."

"Finn sacrificed himself for the greater good."

"In one fell swoop you've banished Cthulhu from the Dreamlands, removed the king from power, and activated your blade, all so you could wield control over the residents here, and continue to spread chaos in the waking world while my son, one of the most powerful beings in existence, is trapped in the skies above, protecting you."

Nyarlathotep clapped his hands in a slow and uniformed beat. "And none of it would have been possible without you, Frances Smith. Thank you for releasing Cthulhu and birthing me a god whom I could mold."

"You're an opportunistic, despicable cheat."

"Cthulhu caused this," Nyarlathotep snapped, gripping the Night-gaunt blade at his side, a not-so-subtle reminder that he was in charge. "It is Cthulhu who killed your husband, who poisoned your son."

"Let me guess, you want me to take care of Cthulhu for you?"

Nyarlathotep leaned forward from his throne. "You do not seek revenge?"

"I'm a mortal."

"Perhaps we can overcome the nightmares and relieve Finn from his post, but not before Cthulhu has been dealt with. I told you to save your strength for what was on the horizon. Cthulhu's physical form will no longer remain idle on R'lyeh. He is the bringer of madness, dear Frances, and he is coming for you."

ABOUT THE AUTHOR

Jonathon T. Cross wears pajama pants in situations that call for semi-formal attire. His reckless disregard for social norms and pant etiquette will be his downfall. He will continue to write books, despite the slack wearing public's disdain for his obtuse behavior. Let it be known that he will never surrender, yield, or otherwise acquiesce to the demands of those who dress for the waking hours.

Made in the USA
Middletown, DE
07 September 2024

60500551R00064